COLD WATERS

LOCUST POINT MYSTERY SERIES, BOOK 12

LIBBY HOWARD

CHAPTER 1

I raced down the sidewalk, the ambulance passing me as I jogged in my pajamas and slippers. It was cold for March, but the early crocuses were beginning to poke through the bits of snow that were crusted here and there on the ground. Not that I could see the crocuses right now. It was still dark out—not even time for Daisy's and my six a.m. yoga, let alone sunrise this time of year. The coffee hadn't finished brewing, and Judge Beck was still sleeping when Daisy's text came in. As soon as I'd gotten the message, I'd barely paused to throw a coat over my pajamas before I'd run out the door.

Emergency at Suzette's.

My mind churned through all the horrible possibilities, fire the foremost in my thoughts. Break-ins weren't all that common in this neighborhood, but not unheard of. The ambulance driving past made me start obsessing on all the horrible things that could need a paramedic response. Had Suzette fallen? Or Olive? Olive stayed over at the cabin that Suzette had inherited from her grandmother far more than

Suzette stayed at her place. They were both rather young for a heart attack, so my thoughts went back to a bad fall.

I jogged past the last Victorian-style home and turned down the long driveway that led to Suzette's house. All of the homes in this neighborhood had once been part of the Hostenfelder farm. The farm had been in Suzette's family since the eighteenth century when her ancestors immigrated from Germany to settle here. The cabin still sat on a couple acres of land, complete with a pond and a few dilapidated outbuildings. Aesthetically it didn't fit in with the ornate nineteenth century homes lined up on what had once been fields and pastures, but the cabin was a part of the neighborhood's history—part of the town's history. And Suzette had never wanted to sell to the developers who continued to wave a tempting amount of money in her face each year.

The cabin's lights were ablaze. I saw Daisy as I was about to climb the porch steps, and she waved for me to follow. I caught up with her just as we rounded the back corner of the house.

"What happened?" I panted like I'd just sprinted five miles instead of the equivalent of three blocks.

"The code that came across the scanner was for some sort of medical emergency. I had to look it up. It's one I've never heard used before."

I gawked at her. "You have a police scanner? And you're listening to it at five o'clock in the morning?"

"The question is why *you* don't have a police scanner, Ms. Private Investigator," Daisy teased. "I listen to it a lot. I like to know what's going on."

"Really? Like traffic stops and the occasional kitchen fire?" I asked. "It's got to be pretty quiet on that police scanner most of the time."

Daisy was a gossip. And now that I thought about it, it really wasn't inconceivable that she'd have a police scanner.

"There's more than you'd think going on around here," Daisy replied. "And I like to know if someone got pulled over drunk, or if a farmer's cows got out and are in the road."

Or if there was a murder. There seemed to be a lot of murders in the last year. I wasn't sure if I just noticed them more because I was working for a private investigation company, or if there had been a new and disturbing increase in violent crime. Maybe I *should* get a police scanner of my own.

"The medical emergency code was the one for a drowning," Daisy continued, her voice softening with worry.

"*Drowning?*" It was thirty degrees out. There was snow on the ground. What the heck would Suzette or Olive be doing that there would be a drowning? I normally would have assumed some sort of shower or bathtub incident, but Daisy was leading me past the backyard and through a field of brown, unmown grass to the pond, where all the first responders seemed to be gathered.

Who in the world would be swimming in the pond in this weather? It was probably still iced over from the bitter cold snap we'd had last week. Had someone been ice skating and fallen through? But I'd seen Suzette's pond, and it wasn't the sort of place for skating or even swimming anymore. The dock had crumbled to a few posts rising from the murky water connected here and there by some broken boards. The edges of the water were thick with briars. The pond itself was full of grass and cattails.

All those thoughts came to an abrupt halt when I saw Suzette sitting on the ground next to the pond, her face in her hands. She was wrapped in the quilt I recognized from her living room sofa. Olive knelt next to her, her arm around Suzette's shoulder.

"I'll go inside and get another blanket," Daisy called out as I ran to the two women.

"What happened?" I asked when I reached them.

"Gus was barking at the back door," Olive explained as she rubbed the other woman's back. "Suzette looked out and saw the paper boy's bike by the rear porch, and got a *feeling*."

Olive worked in finance, but she was also a medium who could contact and speak with ghosts. I saw ghosts—shadowy figures at the edge of my vision—but I'd asked Olive for help a few times when I'd felt a ghost needed to inform me of something that I just wasn't understanding. Outside of Olive and me, I didn't know any of my friends who had more than the occasional ghostly experience. I wasn't sure what sort of feeling Suzette had had, but I certainly understood why others might want to keep any paranormal sensitivities they might have to themselves.

"That darned pond," Suzette said. "I've been meaning to do something about it, but I haven't had the money. I should have it filled in if I can't afford to restore it. I should have done something years ago. That boy—" She burst into tears, burying her face in her hands once more.

Olive wrapped both arms around the other woman and held her tight. "Shush. It's going to be okay. It'll all be okay."

I glanced around, realizing that the paramedics weren't over here administering to Suzette, they were helping someone else—someone bundled in metallic blankets and being hooked up to a variety of medical apparatus. He was young—a teenager with floppy dark hair.

He was someone I recognized.

The paper boy. I gasped. He always tossed my paper into the flower beds, or the bushes, or even on the porch roof in the morning. I'd considered getting the electronic version of our local news over the last two years, but I liked holding the actual paper in my hands. And I'd liked the young man who rode by on his bike in the dark hours before the sun rose every morning, earning some extra cash. His aim was poor, but he always seemed so industrious and cheerful on the mornings when I was up early enough to see him go by.

What had he been doing in Suzette's pond? A shadowy figure materialized over near a mess of briars, and I lifted a hand to my mouth in horror. It was a ghost. Had the paperboy died? Oh no, how could that have happened? He was just a teenager, so young. But there was a ghost, right there not twenty feet from the spot where the paramedics were working on the boy.

The shadowy spirit shifted, moving closer, and I realized the ghost felt a bit older—possibly in his early twenties. And the ghost itself felt old, as if the tattered spirit had wandered this spot for well over a hundred years.

I shouldn't have been surprised that Suzette's place had ghosts. Her family's long history here meant some of her ancestors were probably reluctant to leave after death. Plus there was a good chance there was a cemetery somewhere nearby as so many old farm families used to bury their dead on their own land. Add to that a traumatic event in the pre-dawn hours, and a ghost was bound to show up.

I was just relieved it wasn't the paperboy's spirit. The absence of that particular ghost gave me hope that maybe this morning would see a happy ending.

Glancing over at Suzette, wet and shivering in the cold, I realized she must have gone into the pond after the boy while Olive dialed 911.

"Here." Daisy re-appeared and wrapped a second blanket around Suzette.

"Should we go inside?" Olive asked. "Suzette, you really should get in a hot shower. There's a pot of coffee ready, bacon in the oven, and some pancakes I'd been cooking before all this happened. Enough for everyone."

"No. Not until..." Suzette lifted her head and nodded over

to where the first responders were working on the paper boy.

"Then I'll bring some coffee out here for all of us," I announced. We could all use a hot beverage, and I probably wasn't the only one desperately in need of caffeine right now.

I headed to the house, noticing Gus barking and jumping up and down at the back storm door, clearly excited about all the commotion outside. Making sure the dog didn't escape, I squeezed inside. I patted the Gus's head, trying to distract him from the events by the pond, then I headed into the kitchen to check on the bacon taking the last, somewhat crispy, pancake out of the skillet. I poured four cups of coffee, adding cream and sugar to the ones for Daisy and Suzette. I was about to go back out to the pond when I saw the paramedics carrying the paperboy on a stretcher to the waiting ambulance. Suzette, Olive and Daisy were heading toward the house. Deputy Miles Perkins was trailing behind them, so I poured another cup of coffee and started a second pot.

Gus ratcheted up his enthusiastic barking and jumping as everyone came into the kitchen. Olive picked the dog up to shush him while I handed Suzette her cup.

Daisy shot Miles a warning glance before shooing Suzette upstairs. "Hot shower and coffee first. Questions can wait until you're warmed up," she said.

Miles nodded in agreement, smiling his thanks as he took the mug I held out to him. Daisy pulled the bacon out of the oven, Olive put some food in Gus's bowl, then set out plates and silverware, as I got the butter and syrup for the pancakes. We'd just sat when Suzette came down the stairs in sweatpants and an oversized T-shirt, her wet hair wound up on top of her head in a towel.

"Fastest shower ever," Olive teased her.

Suzette gave a strained laugh at that. "I didn't want you to eat all the bacon."

Miles rose and pulled out a chair for her and Olive passed her the tray of bacon. I watched Suzette fill her plate with food, noting that the hot shower and coffee had done her a world of good. Her eyes were still red and her face blotchy from crying, but she was no longer shaking with cold.

We all ate in silence. I went in for a second pancake, because Olive's recipe was the best. She used buckwheat flour and some malt which gave the pancakes a wonderfully nutty flavor. I didn't even bother to put syrup on mine. They were so good all they needed was a big pat of butter.

"Are you going to get in trouble for taking so long?" I asked Miles, suddenly realizing that he probably shouldn't be sitting here eating breakfast with us while he was technically on the clock.

"I've got to interview Ms. Suzette for my report," he replied, somewhat defensively.

"It's not like we'd let him stand around and watch while we're eating," Olive commented. "And Suzette needed a hot shower and some breakfast. Nobody should be answering police questions on an empty stomach—especially right after jumping in a freezing pond."

She had a point. I got up and poured us all another round of coffee, then Daisy and I started clearing the dishes.

"Are you ready?" Miles asked Suzette. He waited for her to nod, then took out his pad of paper and a pen.

She took a deep breath, then slowly let it out before speaking. "Olive was making breakfast. I was getting out Gus's food when he started barking and scratching at the back door. It wasn't his usual I've-got-to-go-pee kind of bark. It was the bark he does when there's a delivery guy in the drive or someone's here. I opened the door. Gus shot out, ran down the porch steps, and headed for the back part of the lawn that borders the field and the pond. For a second I thought it was a cat from the neighborhood or some other animal and I called for him to come back."

"Did Gus come back when you called him?" Miles asked as he scribbled notes on his pad of paper.

Suzette shook her head, her smile rueful. "No, he didn't. French Bulldogs have a stubborn streak. The obedience classes are a challenge for poor Gus. He's very good about staying on our property, but he doesn't always come if he's chasing a bird or sniffing something."

As if he wanted to prove Suzette wrong, the Frenchie gave his bowl a final lick, then trotted over to sit attentively beside her, tongue lolling out of his mouth.

Miles chuckled. "I'm glad we're not having that problem with Hutch. He's the star of his obedience class," he added proudly.

I was happy to hear that. Miles had adopted one of the rescue puppies Daisy and I had needed to help place and I was so glad things were working out with his new four-legged friend.

"I stepped outside to go after Gus. Then I saw a bike laying in the grass by the corner of the house. When I saw that bike, I just got a bad feeling." Suzette crossed her arms and hugged her chest. "We've got one of those invisible fence things, so Gus hadn't gone all the way down to the field. But he was standing at the very end of the yard, barking at the pond. So I ran out of the house and in that direction."

Tears sparked in Suzette's eyes. She blinked hard, and took another deep breath.

"Did you hear a shout? Someone calling for help?" Miles asked her.

She shook her head. "No. But I saw a trampled place in the weeds and bushes where someone had recently gone through, so I ran through there. The ice was broken over a section of the pond, and I just knew someone was down there. I jumped in, and let me tell you, that water was so cold it took my breath away. I had yelled for Olive to call 911 as I was running, but as soon as I jumped into the pond, I couldn't have said anything if I wanted to."

"You didn't hear the ice breaking or anything like that before you got down there?" Miles pressed.

Suzette shook her head once more. "Maybe he fell through when I was still in the house and Gus heard it and started barking? If that's when he went in, I wouldn't have heard him if he called out for help."

Suzette sipped her coffee as Miles wrote, waiting for him look up at her before continuing.

"So, like I said, I ran down to the pond and I saw where the brush had been flattened and where the ice had been broken. I pushed past all the briars and grasses, and dove in. The water was freezing cold and dark. There's all sorts of vegetation growing up through the water. That pond is a mess and has been for the last fifty odd years. The mud sucks your feet in clear to your knees in some places, and it's easy to get tangled in the grasses and cattails. We used to swim there when I was little, but Grandpa made us stop, saying it was too dangerous. They never had the money to fix the pond." She paused and wiped away a tear. "And I haven't either. I haven't even had the money to get the back three acres mowed like I try to do at least once a year."

Three acres? I had only thought Suzette owned the two acres around the old farmhouse cabin. I'd not realized she also owned the field behind the pond that was thick with overgrown bushes and saplings.

"This place is falling apart," she continued. "I can't keep up with it, and now someone may have…may have died."

Olive reached out and put a hand on her shoulder. "It's not your fault, Suzette."

"It is." She swiped at another tear. "I should have at least come up with the money to fill that pond in, or sold it and the back three acres to one of those developers so *they* could fill it in. I just…I kept hoping I could save enough to restore it. I've got pictures of my grandparents and parents fishing from the dock, swimming, floating on rafts. We used to have ducks and geese there as well. I didn't want to give up on the old pond, but if kids are going to sneak over to swim in it and almost drown…"

"Nobody wants to swim in an ice-covered pond in March," Daisy pointed out. "If kids are going to sneak somewhere to swim, it'll be in that gorgeous new pool the Wilson's put in last summer, not your muddy, weed-filled pond, Suzette. No offense to your family watering hole."

Suzette laughed. "No offense taken. You're right. Nobody in their right mind would want to go swimming in my overgrown pond in March. But why was that boy out there, then?"

Miles waved his pen. "Let's put that on hold and go back to your account of what happened. You jumped into the pond…?"

"I jumped in and started feeling around in the water because I couldn't see anything. The pond is iced over, but it wasn't thick and looking up I could tell where the ice was broken and the weeds trampled because it was lighter in those patches. I came up a few times for air. I think it was the second or third time I dove down, I felt something. Like an arm or a leg. I grabbed hold with both hands and just swam like crazy." Suzette let out her breath in a whoosh. "I'm not the most athletic woman in the world, but I've always been a good swimmer. I don't know how I managed, but I got him out of the pond and started to do CPR on him. Olive must have let Gus inside when she called 911 because I remember not hearing him barking as I pulled the boy out of the water.

She came running down with the quilt and next thing I knew the paramedics where there taking over for me."

"Is he…is he going to be okay?" Olive voiced the questions we'd all been afraid to ask.

"I don't know. He wasn't conscious when they took him away." Miles gave us a worried look as he closed his notepad and put it back in his jacket pocket.

"Can you let us know if you hear something?" Suzette asked. "I know the hospital won't tell me anything, but I just want to know if he's going to be all right. So please tell me."

"That boy has a chance because of you," Miles told her as he stood. "Ms. Suzette, you're a hero this morning. And I'll absolutely let you know as soon as I hear something from the hospital."

He patted Gus on the head, thanked Olive and Suzette for breakfast, put on his coat and hat, and headed out the door.

Suzette turned to Olive. "Part of me wants to call in sick today at work, but the other part of me thinks it might be good to go in. It might take my mind off everything."

Olive reached down and scratched Gus's head. "This little guy would love to have you hang out here with him for the day, but personally I think it would be better for you to head in to work."

"I agree," Daisy chimed in. "Staying home means you'll just obsess over what happened and worry about that boy."

"Does anyone even know his name?" I wondered, feeling horrible that I didn't. The boy had been delivering my paper for at least three years that I could recall.

"Travis something, I think," Daisy replied.

Travis. I did the math and realized that he probably went to school with Madison, and was most likely in her grade or maybe a year behind her. Did she know him? I suddenly thought of the judge, who was probably getting ready for work and wondering where the heck I was. There would have been a full pot of coffee when he'd got up. Normally Daisy and I would be out back finishing up our yoga, or on our way in for a quick bite and hot drink before getting ready for work ourselves, but instead he'd come down to an empty house, a hungry cat, and a full pot of coffee.

I dug my phone out of my purse, sending him a quick text. "I should probably get back home," I told the others. "Let me know if there's anything I can do to help."

"Can you find out the boy's name for me?" Suzette smiled. "And thank you—both you and Daisy—for racing down here. Having you here really made me feel better."

"I'll figure out who he is and text everyone," I promised. "And I'll see you both at porch happy hour tonight?"

Olive smiled. "We'll be there."

I was glad. After this morning, we *all* could use a glass of wine and the company of friends.

CHAPTER 2

"Is Suzette okay?" Judge Beck asked as he helped me out of my coat. "Good grief, Kay. You ran outside in your pajamas!"

I looked down, a little embarrassed at my current state of dress. I saw him in his pajamas all the time, but I was usually in my yoga clothing when he got up in the morning.

"Suzette will be okay," I told him. "She was really shaken by the whole thing, but didn't seem to be suffering any adverse effects from diving into that freezing pond."

"She's lucky she didn't drown as well. Or get hypothermia." The judge shook his head, and went to hang up my coat. "I wonder what the heck that boy was doing out on her pond, especially in this weather. And before dawn as well."

"We wondered the same thing." I thought of the bike that had still been at the corner of Suzette's house when Daisy and I left. "It was our paperboy. Do you know who he is? Daisy thinks his name is Travis something."

"We have a paperboy?" Judge Beck's eyebrows rose.

"How did you think the paper arrived every day? Magic? Little elves?" I teased.

"I guess I assumed the mail person delivered it. Although now that I think of it, the paper *is* always here long before the mail gets delivered." He tilted his head and eyed me. "Why don't you just read it online?"

"Because I like getting an actual paper. And I like that there's a teenager delivering it." I held up my hands. "It's one of the few jobs young teens can get, and I feel like I'm supporting a young entrepreneur."

"I never thought of it that way." He put a hand on my back, nudging me toward the stairs. "Go shower and get dressed. I'll text Madison and see if she knows who he is. Have you had breakfast?"

I started up the stairs. "Yes I have, thanks. Olive was cooking bacon and pancakes when the whole thing happened. And you know she always cooks for an army."

Judge Beck shook his head and smiled. "She told me once that her family always cooks like they're always expecting company. And I'm jealous about the pancakes. I had toast and a hard-boiled egg for breakfast."

I paused halfway up and turned to face him. "You *should* be jealous. She uses buckwheat and malt. Best pancakes I've ever had."

He groaned. "Thanks for rubbing it in. Now I'm craving pancakes. Think you can convince Olive to give us the recipe?" he asked.

"Oh I'm sure I can."

I made a mental note to text Olive for her recipe, then headed for a shower. I thought about pancakes as I got dressed and tried to decide what baked goods I should make for next week. Madison and Henry came over for their week with us on Sunday and I liked to have something special for their breakfasts. And of course I needed to make enough to bring in so Miles, Molly, and J.T. could have some as well. Maybe I'd make that new recipe for banana chocolate chip muffins. Or those dried cherry scones that Miles really loved.

I also needed to plan food for Taco's gotcha day party Sunday night. When Madison and Henry had found out the date that I'd gotten my cat from the shelter and brought him home, they'd insisted we needed to have a celebration. Some diced roasted chicken would serve as Taco's special treat for the day, but I'd need to make something special for us humans to eat as well. A cake, of course, but what sort of cake?

What the kids didn't realize was that Taco's gotcha day was the same day as Eli's funeral. I'd managed to survive a whole lot of first holidays this year without my husband, including my birthday earlier in the month. The anniversary of his death on Monday had been difficult. I wouldn't have gotten through it if Judge Beck hadn't been so kind and patient with me. He'd made dinners the whole week and had given me the space I'd needed to remember and grieve.

Grief was an odd thing. It came and went like a tide flowing in and out of the shore. There were so many days when I laughed and the world felt bright and full of promise. Then there were days when I missed Eli so much it hurt. The painful days came less often now, but they still came.

I'd made it through last week. I could make it thought Sunday, especially because a year ago at the end of a soul-crushing day, there had been Taco. Bringing him home had been one of the best decisions of my life. I may have been the one who adopted him, but in a way he'd been the one who'd saved me. The supposedly aloof cat who I'd thought would just make this house feel less empty, who would give me another living being to come home to, had become such a part of my life, I just couldn't imagine this being a home without him in it.

I sent a quick text to J.T. and Molly, letting them know I'd be in a little late today, then headed downstairs. I was surprised to see Judge Beck still in the kitchen, instead of on his way to the courthouse.

"Travis Verdino," he told me. "That's the name of our paperboy. Madison knows him, but not very well. He's a sophomore. Quiet. Doesn't do sports or any extracurricular activities like drama or band. She says he also works at the arcade after school. She thinks his family doesn't have a lot of money. Only child. Parents divorced when he was young. Dad lives out of state. It's just him and his mom at their house."

"Oh." I sank into one of the kitchen chairs. "Travis Verdino. I feel so bad that I didn't know his name. I wonder if there's anything we can do to help him and his mom?"

The judge sat across from me, his expression somber. "Madison is on it. She was upset to hear what had happened, and is asking his friends to see what the kids at school can do to help."

"Maybe we can organize a meal train, where we all sign up to deliver a dinner to his family each day?" I suggested. "And take up a collection for gas and grocery store cards? I don't want to presume anything about their finances or insurance, but I think anyone would appreciate not having to cook, as well as having some financial help with food and gas."

"Those are good ideas," Judge Beck commented. "Let's pass around a sign-up sheet and a collection jar tonight at the happy hour."

I nodded. "Suzette feels so horrible about all this. Everyone knows it's not her fault, but to have a child almost drown in her pond...she'll be happy to know we're organizing something to help Travis and his mom."

"On a lighter note," the judge said. "Madison and Henry

are both very excited for Taco's gotcha party on Sunday. I have to warn you that they bought toys. And catnip."

"Is the catnip for us or Taco," I teased. "Should we have some sort of themed dinner? Taco's favorite foods? We can dine on canned tuna and roasted chicken."

The judge made a face. "Let's leave those for Taco and have something else. I don't mind roasted chicken, or tuna, but maybe steaks for the humans instead?"

"Tacos," I told him, trying to keep my expression serious. "In honor of Taco, we should have tacos."

"On Sunday?" He put a hand to his chest in mock horror. "I thought tacos could only be consumed on Tuesday."

"This is an exception to that rule." I could no longer hold back a smile. "I'm just kidding. Steaks it is."

"Too late. You've proclaimed it Taco's taco day. Besides the kids would think it was hysterical. Henry told me he's making a cake shaped like a cat for dessert. We're probably all going to need to wear party hats—Taco included."

I laughed. "I've got no problem wearing a party hat. Honestly, I think this all sounds like a lot of fun. I'm excited for Sunday."

"Me too." He got up and moved around to my side of the table, putting his arm around my shoulders. "How are you doing? I know this week was hard for you. Is there anything I can do to help?"

My breath caught. "Everything you do helps. Just having you here with me helps. Thank you for understanding and being patient."

"Oh, Kay." He bent down and kissed the top of my head. "You were married to Eli for decades. You loved him. You still love him. I understand that, and I understand your grief. I'll be as patient as I need to be."

I lifted my face to look at him. "I'm better today. Although this morning at Suzette's gave me quite a scare."

He nodded. "We'll talk more about what we can do to help Travis and his mom tonight. In the meantime I need to get to work."

"Me too." I pushed the chair back and stood, but the judge didn't budge from his spot beside me.

Instead he leaned forward and kissed me. It was one of those kisses that made me wish we both could play hooky from work and spend the day in each other's arms. But we were adults with responsibilities, so I kissed him back, and sighed with regret when he pulled away.

"Later," he promised.

I smiled, my heart pounding a little harder at the thought.

"Later," I agreed.

CHAPTER 3

"Sorry I'm late," I called out as I came through the door. J.T. wasn't at his desk in the back section of the office, so he was most likely over at the courthouse. Molly was at her little desk, off to the side of where mine stood.

The girl spun around on her chair. "I heard all the commotion on the scanner this morning. Someone drowned in Suzette's pond?"

"Almost drowned. He's at the hospital. Although technically I think anytime they have to revive someone, they call it a drowning," I told her.

Unlike with Daisy, I wasn't surprised that Molly had a police scanner. She'd taken to listening to it while at home, claiming it was a work-related activity. J.T. had promptly told her he wasn't paying overtime for her scanner hobby. I kind of understood her line of reasoning, though. Knowing what sort of bail bonds work or potential investigations might be coming our way *would* be beneficial. And then, there was the whole curiosity thing. My best friend Daisy was in the know as far as what was happening in our town and county, but Molly had also become my go-to for what the first responders had been busy with for the last twenty-four hours. Usually it was something like a four-wheeler accident on Hammond Road, or that Mildred Purcell's trash fire had gotten out of hand again, but occasionally Molly had been able to give us the heads-up about a robbery or drug arrest in Milford, or a domestic violence arrest in Beaver Falls.

Molly's eyes widened. "What the holy heck was someone doing in Suzette's pond early morning in March? It's freezing out there. There's still snow on the ground from Wednesday. Were they trying to ice skate or something and fell in?"

I held up my hands. "No one has any idea what he was doing out there. I doubt it was ice skating. The pond is covered in marsh grass and cattails. And anyone who skates knows it hasn't been consistently cold enough for there to be a thick layer of ice."

"Well, he sure as heck wasn't going for a quick swim." Molly frowned. "Was it something he did on a dare? I swear it seems guys will do the craziest things if one of their buddies dares them to."

I hadn't thought about that. People did those polar bear plunges into the lake every year, even though that was for charity donations.

"It might have been a dare," I mused. "The boy who almost drowned was our paperboy. Travis Verdino. He's a sophomore at Locust Point High, so I'm guessing he's probably fifteen years old."

Molly slowly shook her head. "Fifteen. I get chills thinking that he almost died."

"I don't think he's completely out of the woods yet," I told her. "Thankfully Gus was barking at the back door so Suzette went out, saw the boy's bike and got a bad feeling. She ran down there, jumped in still wearing her pajamas, and pulled him out."

"She saved his life," Molly said, echoing my thoughts. "Thank goodness she ran out there or he surely would have died. I guess when he regains consciousness, he'll say why he did such a crazy thing."

"I guess." I prayed that Travis Verdino did regain consciousness. And I prayed he didn't suffer any long-lasting effects of his near-drowning as well.

Sitting down at my desk, I got to work researching a repossession J.T. was going to need to handle later today. I was glad he was the one sneaking out to people's jobs and homes and grabbing their cars instead of me. I always felt bad about this side of our business. It felt kind of like stealing to go grab someone's vehicle while they were at work or eating dinner, but in all fairness the loan company had given them plenty of notice, and if they hadn't been making their payments for this long, then the finance people did have a right to take action.

It wasn't just my guilt over snatching up someone's vehicle for non-payment that made me glad J.T. handled this end of the business, it was that he frequently had people screaming at him, chasing him down the road, or even confronting him and threatening violence as he tried to take the car. I'd already been on the wrong side of a gun too many times in the last year to want to risk getting shot over a three-year-old Hyundai Sonata.

Around noon Miles came in. Instead of heading straight for the coffee area and looking for any baked goods I might have made, the deputy headed towards Molly and me, extending a paper bag from each hand.

"I come bearing gifts," he teased. "Lunch is on me, ladies."

I thanked him and grabbed the bag, absolutely starving.

Inside was a turkey club, a small bag of chips, and a carefully wrapped pickle spear.

"Thank you, Miles," Molly said, biting into her pickle.

"I figured you'd need the fuel. I ran into J.T. at the station. He's got a load of work he's about to dump on the two of you in the next week or two."

"Wonderful," I drawled, opening my bag of chips. "What's he got—more bail bonds research? A big case? Are we expanding into the next state?"

"Process serving." Miles shrugged. "He'll give you all the details whenever he gets in. Or maybe he'll just spring it on you in a week or so."

"Process serving," I repeated with some dread. Great. This would be just like the car repossession thing, only we'd be chasing down people and trying to serve them paperwork to appear in court instead of taking away their cars and trucks. We wouldn't be serving criminal summonses or search warrants like police officers did, so hopefully there wouldn't be as much risk of being shot at or chased down the road.

And at least we wouldn't have to drive off with someone's car.

"How is Violet? How are the wedding plans? Have the two of you set a date yet?" Molly asked Miles.

The deputy and Violet had gotten engaged over Valentine's Day, right after he'd adopted one of the puppies Daisy and I were finding homes for. I was *so* excited for their upcoming wedding. Young people, starting their life together, made me feel all romantic and mushy inside.

"A year from June." Miles rolled his eyes. "I wanted *this* June, but Violet says churches and reception places and catering companies are all booked up a year in advance and she doesn't want a backyard potluck wedding."

"I think a backyard potluck wedding sounds fun," I teased, knowing that I wouldn't have wanted that either at

Violet's age. At sixty-one? A casual, informal celebration sounded great. The idea of a white dress and bridesmaids with a big catered event made me feel exhausted. Just thinking about it made me want to take a nap, but I remembered being in my early twenties, and how planning Eli's and my wedding had been an exciting and all-consuming activity.

"I think a courthouse wedding and hopping on a plane for our honeymoon sounds fun, but Violet wants a big shindig, and if that means we have to wait over a year to get married, then I'll just have to be patient." Miles shrugged.

"I'd want all of my family and friends there on such a special day," Molly said. "I'm siding with Violet on this one."

Miles's shoulders slumped at the word "family" and I gave him a sympathetic glance. I knew he wasn't thrilled with Violet's less-than-law-abiding relatives, but that was something he'd had to accept when he'd started dating her. Still, it would be difficult for a sheriff's deputy to have in-laws who'd done, or were currently doing, time.

"Well, she definitely wants her family there. *All* of her family. And she wants her youngest sister to be a bridesmaid," he said.

"How *is* Peony?" I asked, knowing Violet was one of the few family members who'd kept in touch with her sister after she'd been convicted and sentenced for her role in Holt Dupree's death.

"Peony is up for an early release. It looks like she might be out of the detention facility and on parole as early as next month," Miles commented, sounding none too happy about that for some reason.

"That's great news!" Molly exclaimed, clearly missing the signs of Miles's dismay. "I'm so happy for her. Violet must be excited to be having her sister back home again."

Miles flinched, and I suddenly understood that there was

more to this situation than his soon-to-be sister-in-law being released from the juvenile detention facility.

"She's moving in with Violet, isn't she?" I asked softly.

He sighed. "Peony's family won't let her come home, which is a whole lot of people living in glass houses and throwing stones as far as I'm concerned. There isn't one among them except for Violet who hasn't been arrested at one time or another, and plenty have served time. But they've decided Peony's crime, and probably the widespread news coverage of it, isn't something they want to be associated with."

"And Peony is only sixteen," I added.

"She'll be seventeen this summer, but has no job, no money, and will be on parole, so it's not like she can file for emancipation. Plus they're not going to let her out early if she doesn't have somewhere to stay. Conditions of her parole are going to be having a fixed address, getting a job or attending school full-time, and staying this side of the law." Miles blew out a breath. "The rest of her family has pretty much disowned her. And you know how Violet is."

"She has a big heart," I agreed. "And she believes in second chances. So should you. As a sheriff's deputy, you should have faith in rehabilitation, and that criminals who've paid for their crimes can become productive members of society once more."

"I want to believe that, but I'm a realist and the recidivism rate of criminals isn't a pretty number." Miles ran a hand through his hair. "I don't mind Violet helping her little sister. I just don't want to see her getting tangled up in Peony's troubles. I don't want them to keep Violet from all the things she wants to do with her life—things that might require her to have a security clearance and a spotless record. And, self-ishly I'll admit, I don't want Violet's little sister staying at her house and dampening the romantic fire, if you know what I mean."

Molly snorted. "So bring her to your own house, where the only thing dampening your fire is Hutch."

I bit back a smile, thinking that if anything, an adorable puppy would only enhance the romantic fire.

"I would, but my place is…well, it's a guy's apartment. Besides, Violet likes to have her stuff handy in the morning when she wakes up, and she likes to cook with her own pans and stuff. I tend to bring Hutch over and we stay at her house."

Molly stared at him. "Dude, get your act together. Violet should have a drawer in your dresser and room in your closet as well as a toothbrush in your bathroom. Go buy all the toiletries and products she likes and keep them at your house. Buy the food she likes. Buy things like matching dishes and throw pillows and stuff. Because I'm telling you right now, her sister is moving in and if you ever want to do the mattress mambo on the regular again, you'll need to make your apartment a place where she wants to stay."

Miles looked to me and I held up my hands. "I agree with Molly here. You do need to step up here or get used to trying to spark that romantic fire with Peony walking in and out of the living room every five minutes."

He shuddered. "Okay, okay. I'm going over to her house tonight. I'll take pictures of all her shampoo and stuff and go shopping in the morning."

Molly rolled her eyes. "You've been dating how long, and you don't know what shampoo she uses yet?"

"It's in a white bottle. I think it might be Paul Mitchell or something, but even if I get the brand right there's probably eight different types and they all look the same." He shrugged. "It's shampoo. I pour a bit in my hand, and that's it. I don't really think about what brand it is."

"It's because his hair is all of half an inch long," I told Molly.

"He probably doesn't even need to condition," she replied.

"Okay, okay," Miles groused. "I get the idea. Pay more attention to stuff that she likes, the little comforts she fills her home with, and recreate that at my place."

"Exactly," I told him. "But it might be a good idea to let her come with you to pick out the throw pillows and dishes. She'll think it's fun, and that way you won't inadvertently buy something hideous."

He nodded. "Good idea. Thanks, guys…er, ladies."

"You're welcome." Molly turned back to her computer, a smug smile on her face.

"While you're here, have you heard anything about Travis Verdino? Do you know how he's doing?" I asked, thinking once more of the near tragedy that I couldn't seem to get out of my mind this morning.

"How did you find out his name?" Miles asked.

"I'm an ace private investigator, that's how." I laughed at his astonished expression. "Actually the judge texted his daughter and asked her. He's a teen. She's a teen. Locust Point isn't that big, so he figured Madison went to school with him and would know him."

Miles nodded. "That's still some good detective work, Miss Kay. But I'm afraid I don't have any news, good or bad, on his condition. The doctors said with drownings, they usually keep the patient sedated for a while because of the possibility of brain swelling. They told me it was lucky Miss Suzette was there to pull him out and to start CPR. Evidently in unattended drownings or cases where CPR isn't done right away, the survival rate is only about eight percent."

That sobered me right up. "But Suzette *was* there. And she did CPR on him. So there has to be a better chance of survival, right?"

Miles shrugged. "We don't know how long he was under before she pulled him out. It's just going to take time to see how he responds. He might not make it. He might pull through but have neurological injuries. He could survive but end up with pneumonia or an infection because of the bacteria in the water. He could survive and face long-term lung issues due to scarring."

"Oh." I brushed away sudden tears. "His poor mother must be a wreck."

Miles nodded. "Before I sat down with you all at Suzette's place, I had someone call the newspaper for the boy's information, and sent an officer over to the house to deliver the news and offer to take his mother to the hospital. I thought she might not be fit to drive, and no one should get that kind of news over the phone."

I nodded approvingly. Miles was young, but he took his job seriously and I could see a great future for him. He was one of the good guys—one of the people who saw policing not just as crime response, but as a community service.

I promised Miles there'd be some baked goodies in the office on Monday. He patted his stomach, vowed to make time to visit, then headed out. I watched him leave, a fond smile on my face.

"Violet is a lucky woman," I mused.

"Miles is a lucky man," Molly responded.

I agreed, my smile fading as I thought about Violet's sister. "I feel really bad for Peony. I was never happy with her sentencing. She had no prior record. It was involuntary manslaughter. She had no idea Holt was taking that other medication."

"But she drugged him," Molly pointed out. "When you give someone an illegal substance, intending to blackmail them…that's not something that deserves only a slap on the wrist. Plus Holt was a celebrity. He was a talented young man, whose life was cut short because Peony wanted to make some easy money. I think less than a year in juvie is actually getting off light."

I sighed, knowing Molly was right. But I'd been the one who'd discovered what Peony had done, who convinced her to turn herself in and come clean. She'd been one of Madison's friends, no matter how uncomfortable Judge Beck had felt about that situation. And with her family… She'd grown up thinking petty theft and breaking the law for a quick buck was just a part of life.

But Violet had broken that cycle. Violet had gone to college, gotten her degree, and had a good job at the courthouse. She was engaged to a sheriff's deputy, looking into enrolling in a master's degree program online. Last week at happy hour, she'd even confessed to me that she was applying to the FBI for a job. I'd had my fingers firmly crossed for her ever since, thinking it would be an amazing opportunity for her to work in a federal financial crimes group. They'd be lucky to have such a talented and smart employee.

If Violet had made a success of her life in spite of her family's history, I had hope for Peony—even though she'd had a rocky start. I'd meant what I'd said to Miles about redemption and second chances. Peony had come clean about her crime. She'd expressed sincere regret. She'd served her sentence. Shouldn't this be the perfect opportunity for her to turn her life around? And how better to do that than by living with the one sister who had taken a different path than the rest of her family?

Molly spun her chair around to look at me. "I absolutely get wanting to take care of family. Hunter is my brother and I'd do anything for him. So I understand Violet letting Peony move in with her. Where else does the girl have to go?"

"But?" I asked, knowing there was a "but" coming.

"But Violet's engaged. To a cop. She's planning a wedding, applying for a master's program. I know she's got big plans for her career. I hate to see Peony throw a wrench in all that."

I thought about that a second. "Then we need to make sure no wrenches, or other tools, are thrown. First, Peony needs to go back to school."

Molly grimaced. "Wouldn't that be hard for her? I can see the other kids either shunning her or giving her grief for her conviction. Getting in fights at school, and dealing with the stress being blackballed isn't going to help her. Maybe she should just get her GED instead?"

I nodded. "True, but I think that needs to be Peony's decision. She had friends before, and I know some of the kids at school were keeping in contact with her—Madison included. If she just had a handful of friends at school, then I think she could stick it out. Everything would all blow over in a few weeks, hopefully."

Molly wrinkled her nose. "True. I still think the GED is a better idea, but it should be her choice."

"And she needs a job," I added. "She needs to earn spending money, maybe start saving. She needs to get job experience for when she graduates next year. Or when she gets her GED."

"Not a lot of places hire convicted felons," Molly pointed out. "Especially ones as notorious as Peony Smith. Everyone knew about the Holt Dupree murder. No one is going to want to give her a job."

"Then she'll just have to take whatever she can get," I pointed out. "Or maybe do volunteer work for a while until she's reintegrated into the community and people feel better about hiring her."

"I'm still thinking her best bet would be to get her GED, then move somewhere people might not recognize her. Iowa. Or Texas," Molly suggested.

"Kind of hard to do that when you're out on parole and have no money, and are sixteen years old," I reminded her. But Molly was right. It would be a hard road for Peony. Maybe I could help on the job front though. Daisy worked with at-risk teens. She might know of places that would be willing to hire a teenage girl just coming out of juvenile detention—even one whose crimes had been as notorious as Peony's. And luckily we had time. Miles had said the girl wouldn't be released until next month. That gave us at least four weeks to line up some options—options that hopefully Peony would consider.

CHAPTER 4

J.T. had taken to letting me leave work early on Fridays to prep for the porch happy hour. It wasn't really such a favor as I was now a salaried employee and still had to get my work done even with the increased flexibility in my work hours. I felt a bit guilty skipping out at three, especially given that I'd been late coming in, but the thick clutch of folders in my bag with my laptop reassured my work ethic that I'd be more than making up the time this weekend.

In addition to my happy hour prep, I wanted to stop by the hospital to check on Travis. And I kind of wanted to be gone before J.T. came back to the office, just in case he wanted me to spend my weekend knocking on doors and delivering summonses.

The man at the hospital receptionist's desk told me that Travis had just been moved from the emergency room to ICU, and that only immediate family would be allowed to visit. Hoping to find his mother in the waiting area, I headed to that floor, stopping by the nurses' desk when I saw the waiting area was empty.

"Hi." I smiled at the woman behind the desk. "I know I can't visit Travis Verdino, but I'm hoping to speak with his mother. My friend was the one who pulled her son out of the pond this morning, and I was thinking I'd get a group of people together from the neighborhood to deliver food and maybe take up a collection to buy gift cards to help the family."

"Oh, that's so sweet." The woman glanced down the hall, then back at me. "She's in with him now. I'll tell her you're here, Ms…"

"Carrera," I told her. "I'll be in the waiting room over here. Tell her there's no hurry. And if she'd rather not leave him, I can always give you my information to pass on to her."

The woman stood. "I'm sure she could benefit from a little break. She's hasn't left her son's side since he was in the ER."

I grimaced, torn between feeling like I was intruding on this family crisis, and wanting to offer help as well as my sympathy and prayers for Travis's recovery. Heading to the waiting room, I sat, determined not to take too much of this woman's time.

After about ten minutes, Travis's mom appeared. She was a short, angular woman with her black curly hair pulled back in a messy bun. There were shadows under her dark brown eyes, and her business suit was rumpled. I looked at the charcoal gray pants and silky shirt and realized that she'd probably been getting ready for work when the police came by to deliver the news.

"Ms. Verdino." I stood and I shook her hand. "I'm Kay Carrera. Travis delivers my papers, and I know some of his schoolmates. I live down the street from the pond…"

My voice trailed off before I said "where he was found," thinking she'd know what pond I was talking about and that it wouldn't be kind to remind her how close her son had come to dying.

She ran a smoothing hand over her suit and gave me a wan smile. "Thank you for coming by. Do you know the woman who saved Travis? The one who lives in the cabin with the pond? The officer who brought me to the hospital told me what happened. If that woman hadn't realized something was wrong, hadn't gone in that freezing water in her pajamas to pull Travis out, then sat there soaking wet in the cold, performing CPR on him, I wouldn't have a son to worry over right now. I owe her everything."

She swiped a tear away and I found myself doing the same. Suzette blamed herself for what had happened, and I knew she'd been afraid Travis's mother would blame her as well.

"She's a friend of mine," I told the woman. "And she's very worried about him. We all are. How is Travis doing?"

She sighed, glancing behind her and down the hallway. "He's stable. He's still on oxygen, and they still have him sedated and wrapped in warming blankets, but the doctor seemed optimistic just now. There's worry about irritation to his lung tissue, and infection. Pneumonia is also a concern, but so far there hasn't been the brain swelling they feared there would be. They'll reduce the sedation tomorrow sometime, and we're all praying he wakes up without any lasting cognitive damage."

I let out a breath. "That's wonderful news. I know some of the kids in his school are planning something, but I wanted to offer the assistance of our neighborhood as well. I was thinking of taking up a collection for grocery store and gas gift cards. Or something else. Maybe cash. Maybe a Go-Fund-Me to help with medical costs?"

I squirmed, uncomfortable with this whole thing. I'd been on the other side of this situation ten years ago. When Eli had his accident, we'd been comfortable financially, so the assistance I'd needed at the time had been meals, prayers, and companionship. As years went by and finances dwindled, I'd cherished every offer of groceries, and house cleaning—and cash. As humiliating as it had been for me to accept an envelope with a handful of twenties in it, the money had been much needed. It had all gone toward medical equipment that our insurance didn't cover, that extra session of physical therapy, or an emergency repair for my old car. Things like household maintenance and clothing had fallen far down the priorities list when faced with bills for items and services that could make Eli's life more comfortable. I'd desperately needed help and that had never lessened in the ten years since Eli's accident. It hadn't ended with his death either. But no matter how much I'd needed assistance, it hadn't been easy to accept it.

"That's too much," she protested. "I can't...it's too much. We'll be okay."

I reached out to touch her arm, then withdrew. "Please. You need to concentrate on Travis and on yourself and not be worried about things like being able to pay the medical bills, or gas, or groceries, or your mortgage because you had to take time off work to care for your son. Let us help. We've all been there—*I've* been there. Give us the opportunity to pay back for all the people who helped us out when we've had a crisis."

She made a choking noise, covering her face with her hands. Her shoulders heaved for a few seconds, then she lifted her face, took a deep breath, and blinked away the tears.

"Thank you so much. Anything you can do—gift cards or payment to the hospital on our behalf. You're right. Anything at all will really help. I need...I need to just stay here and concentrate on my son."

I smiled. "I'll drop by the hospital tomorrow afternoon to check on Travis and bring by some gift cards. We also wanted to do a meal train for you. I know Travis probably isn't going home for a few days at least, but when he gets home it might be nice to have meals delivered for the both of you for a few weeks."

That had been really valuable when Eli had come home from the hospital. I'd been so busy with getting the bed and other equipment set up, dealing with the insurance, the doctors, and the therapists, that cooking food had been the last thing on my mind. If it hadn't been for my friends delivering meals, I would have lived for weeks on chips and crackers.

"That isn't necessary," she hurriedly replied. Then she thought for a second. "But it would be appreciated. I don't know what his recovery will be like, or what I'll need to do for him when he's released from the hospital. Not having to cook would let me focus on him and his recovery."

I smiled. "Then I'll need to have your address as well as any food preferences, dislikes, or allergies. I'll coordinate everything and swing by tomorrow to let you know what's going on. Maybe I can relieve you here while you run home for a shower and a change of clothes? I assume you're going to spend the night here."

"Thanks. I did plan on staying here tonight—as long as Travis is in the ICU and not conscious, I don't feel like I can leave." She ran a hand through her hair. "When the police came by I was getting ready for work. I usually head out just about the time that Travis is finishing up his route, so I didn't worry when he wasn't home yet. When the officer told me what had happened, I followed him straight to the hospital and haven't been back home. Thank goodness the coffee maker has an automatic shutoff," she laughed weakly.

"I'll come by around noon tomorrow," I promised.

She gave me her address and phone number and I did the same. "Thank you, Ms. Carrera," she said, for the first time seeming to relax.

"Please call me Kay," I told her.

She nodded and smiled. "Then please, call me Linda."

"Linda." I picked up my purse, shoving my phone back inside. "You'll text me with any updates? If you have time, that is."

"Oh, absolutely. And please tell your friend how grateful I am that she saved my son. I'd like to thank her personally. If she can come over to my house once Travis is out. I'm sure he'd like to thank her as well."

"Suzette would love that. I'll pass the offer along."

I headed out to the hospital parking lot with a lot on my mind. It felt good knowing that the community would come together to help Travis and his family, but there was one more person who needed us. Suzette was feeling guilty about this whole thing even though it wasn't her fault that the teen had gone into her pond and nearly drowned. I knew she'd struggled financially since inheriting the house and land from her grandmother, and that the needed repairs and maintenance on the old property were more than she could handle on her salary. I had no idea how much it would cost for pond restoration, or even just a fence to secure the area, but maybe a fundraiser could help. I kept thinking that if Suzette had enough money to do some of the needed repairs, she wouldn't need to worry about all these things.

Just as we needed to help Travis and his family, we also needed to help Suzette. And I planned to make sure our friends, family, and community were there for both of them.

CHAPTER 5

Iraced home to get set up in time for our weekly porch happy hour. Taco was thrilled at my arrival and immediately informed me that I was late feeding him.

"It's not even four thirty," I complained as he jumped up, batting my legs with soft paws and meowing plaintively. "Fine, fine. Even though I know you'll probably get plenty of snacks at the happy hour."

Our end-of-week celebration had grown substantially in the last year. What had originally started out with me, Daisy, Kat, and Suzette, now included Violet and Miles, Olive, Molly and occasionally her brother Hunter, Matt Poffenberger, and, of course, the judge. Other neighbors sometimes stopped by, and with the adoption of the puppies Daisy and I had been taking care of, we had a pack of young dogs as well. Taco wasn't the only four-legged attendee, and his initial annoyance with all the yappy canines quickly vanished when he realized puppies were good at knocking stuff off tables— stuff that he enjoyed eating.

All of the pups would quickly retreat with a hiss and a glare from Taco, letting the cat enjoy the spoils of war. The only two dogs that seemed to get a jump on the cat when it came to the scraps were Olive and Suzette's French Bulldog, Gus, and Daisy's terrier-mix rescue, Lady.

Needless to say, attempts to reduce Taco's weight had been a failure. I was pretty sure I'd be in for a scolding at the vet next month when I took him in for his checkup.

Pouring some food in my cat's bowl to keep him occupied, I grabbed the two quiches I'd made yesterday and quickly stuck them in the oven to warm. Then I pulled out the wine—two bottles of white and two of red—as well as a six pack of beer for Matt and the judge, and a handful of flavored non-alcoholic seltzers that were for those of my friends under the age of twenty-one as well as some of the neighbors who might decide not to partake in an alcoholic beverage tonight.

All of this was courtesy of Judge Beck, who'd taken to stocking up a veritable liquor store downstairs in the recreational room of my basement. He also footed the grocery bill for snacks, claiming that not only did he have a responsibility to chip in for the happy hour costs, but that his kids probably ate ninety-percent of the leftovers. In reality he did far more than just chip in. I appreciated it, because although my neighbors and friends did bring food and drink contributions, most of the consumables came out of my fridge. And given my tight budget, our guests would have been eating chips, dip, and drinking from a gallon jug of generic wine if the judge hadn't opened up his wallet.

I knew he enjoyed these shindigs just as much as I did, and that he relished his role as co-host, so I never protested and gratefully let him pay for it all.

The first things I took out to the porch were a heavy glass bowl, and a clipboard with a few sheets of paper attached. Scrawling the word "donations for Travis" on a notecard, I set the bowl on a table and propped the note up next to it.

Then I filled out the blank paper on the clipboard to make a sign-up list for the meal train. That done, I ran back in for the food. Grabbing the bags of chips and the basket that held the paper plates, napkins, and plastic cutlery, I went back outside to find Daisy standing on a chair and lighting the porch heater.

"I'll be so glad when we're done with this thing," she complained.

"Me too." Even though the heater that the judge had purchased allowed us to continue our Friday tradition through the winter, I'd welcome warmer weather. The day I stored this thing in the garage, would be the day I *truly* celebrated spring.

"Did you hear we're supposed to have another cold snap?" Daisy asked as she climbed off the chair. "They're predicting snow flurries tomorrow."

I groaned. "It's March, for Pete's sake. Enough already. My crocuses and daffodils won't make it through a hard freeze."

"They're hardy enough," Daisy countered. "And the snow will insulate them. Hopefully this is winter's last hurrah and we'll see some warmer weather ahead next week."

I set the basket and the chips on the table, then dragged the big metal tub that we used for the wine and other drinks around from the side yard. Daisy went back to her car where I saw her retrieving an enormous cheese tray. Running back inside, I lugged out a bag of ice—as if we needed it in this weather—and two of the wine bottles.

By the time I had all the drinks organized and some wine glasses set out on a table, Daisy had organized the food into a lovely spread. The chips were in a bowl. Her cheese platter was next to an assortment of crackers and a little dish with gourmet olives.

"I picked up some cookies from the bakery," she told me,

holding open a box. "Chocolate with toffee chips, and sugar cookies with Madagascar vanilla and macadamia nuts."

My mouth watered. There were a few cars already pulling up to the curb, and I knew the quiches in the oven were ready to come out, so I snatched a cookie out of the box and ran back inside.

When I came back with the two quiches—one bacon and gruyere, and the other spinach parmesan, Matt was helping arrange the chairs he'd carried to the front of the porch from around back while Daisy opened up a beer for him. Kat was walking up the driveway with a bottle of wine in each hand, and Molly and Hunter were getting out of their car, Starsky rolling on the grass at the end of his leash.

Molly had fallen in love with the solid black pup, who'd been the chunkiest and most mellow of the litter. At the time of the pups' adoption, I'd been calling them hound/retriever mixes, but it was clear that whatever Starsky's parentage had been, it was most likely part sloth. Honestly that worked out well for Molly and Hunter who lived in an apartment. Their pup rarely barked and had zero separation anxiety. She'd told me he loved nothing more than going into his crate, snuggling up with the blankets, and chewing on a toy.

I waved to them, then started pouring glasses of wine and getting out the sodas. Before I knew it, my porch was packed with people, all laughing, eating, drinking, and enjoying the end of the work week for those of us who had nine-to-five, Monday through Friday jobs.

There was already a good amount of money and change in the bowl I'd set out for donations to go to Travis and his mom. I'd eyed it, planning to buy gift cards in the morning, then go over to the hospital at lunch time. I'd continue to request monetary donations through the week, but it was the sign-up list for the meal train that I was really keeping an eye on.

"Is this the boy who almost drowned in Suzette's pond?" Kat asked as she dropped a ten in the jar and wrote her name on the meal train list. "What in the world was he thinking going out on that pond like that?"

"I wonder if he saw a cat or a stray dog out on the ice or an animal that had partially fallen through the ice, and was trying to help it," Violet mused.

"Or perhaps he saw something else out there," Daisy added. "Suzette said people used to throw junk in the pond. When she was a kid, she once pulled an old boot up when she was fishing. Maybe Travis saw something sticking out of the ice and the brush, and went in to get it."

I couldn't imagine a teen would risk going out onto thin ice to yank a boot out of the pond. Then I thought of Henry and his love of all things antique as well as things that were just plain old. Some kids were curious and probably *would* want to go investigate something sticking up through the ice. But it would have to have been a large item for Travis to have seen it from the front of the house where his paper route had taken him. Anything that large, Suzette would have seen days before and probably hauled out herself.

"Molly thought that maybe he'd done it on a dare, but I guess we won't know anything more until he regains consciousness," I commented.

"I just hope when he does regain consciousness that he doesn't have any lasting damage." Kat shook her head. "He's lucky Suzette got to him when she did."

"Speaking of Suzette, where is she?" Daisy asked looking around. "And Olive?"

Judge Beck hadn't arrived yet either, but that wasn't uncommon for him. But Olive had a nine-to-five, and the sort of job where it wasn't a big deal for her to cut out a little early on a Friday. Sometimes Suzette got held up at work, but usually she was here by now.

As if on cue, Suzette's car pulled up to the curb. She got out, dressed in jeans with her parka zipped and the hood up. Friday was business casual at her office, but jeans didn't fit that relaxed dress code, so I assumed Suzette had ended up taking the day off after all.

As she crossed the lawn and climbed the steps, I moved to pour her a glass of wine. The poor woman looked like she needed a drink.

The ladies all rallied around her, asking how she was and expressing admiration over her heroic actions this morning. Suzette dropped the hood of her parka, smoothed a hand through her disheveled hair, and gratefully took the glass of wine I held out.

"I just came from Smyth and Long Homes," she announced. "Nothing is decided yet, but I wanted to explore my options. There's just too much to do as far as restoring the house and property, and after this morning...I don't think the pond is safe. If I can't afford to make it safe, then maybe I need to sell everything except the house and the immediate property around it."

Everyone fell silent at that. I reached out and gave Suzette a quick hug around her shoulders. "It's always good to think through all the alternatives. And no one would blame you for selling some of your land. Every one of us living along this street has a house that was built on land your family once owned. We wouldn't be here if your family hadn't made the decision to sell some of their farm a hundred and fifty years ago."

She nodded. "I know, and I love having neighbors—I love having *you* all as neighbors. Honestly, I couldn't have managed a huge working farm. I'm not sure I can manage what I've got now."

"I didn't even know you owned that land behind the pond," I confessed to her.

It was a weird block of land. The field bordered a line of modern split-level and ranch-style houses along the back and right sides, Suzette's property in the front, and the rear of another farm to the left. All these years, I'd always assumed that patch of land belonged to the other farm.

"I do own it." She sighed. "But it's just a field of weeds and brambles and saplings that I pay to have mowed when I've got the spare cash. If I'm not going to do anything with it, then maybe it's time to think of selling those three acres. And the acre with the pond as well."

"It's definitely something you should think about," I told her, hating the thought of Suzette's land being hemmed in by more houses.

"I know." She shrugged. "It's just that I love the history and the legacy of a farm that's been in my family for centuries. I hate to let more of it go."

"Have you looked into getting a loan?" Kat asked tentatively. "I don't know what sort of financial situation you're in or what you're facing as far as repairs on the house and property, but maybe a home equity loan would give you enough cash to do what you need to do and not sell off more of your land?"

Suzette nodded. "I thought about that, but I had some issues a few years back when I was between jobs and I don't have the best credit score right now. Even with the house as equity, I doubt I could get a loan. I tried when I first inherited the property, and the only companies willing to offer me anything were ones that had insanely high interest rates." She took a quick sip of her wine, then sighed. "I've been saving every spare dime and have gotten some much needed work done on the house itself, but there's so much more to do. The house repairs have to come first. Restoring the pond was really low on my priority list, but after this morning…"

"Having your pond restored might not have made a

difference this morning," Daisy said, her voice gentle. "No one knows why that boy decided to go back into your property and try to walk out on a pond with a thin coating of ice. I don't think the condition of your pond had anything to do with his decision."

"She's right," Violet chimed in. "Kids sometimes go into pools and hot tubs, climbing fences when the owners aren't home, bringing booze and partying. Kids still trespass and get in trouble on other people's property when they have fences and have taken precautions."

Kat nodded. "It might not have made a difference even if your pond *was* fixed up and you'd had a fence."

Suzette frowned. "I appreciate what you all are saying, but I've been in that pond a few times over the last few years. The silt at the bottom is like quicksand. And it's easy to get tangled in all the brush, grasses, and cattails. It's deeper than it looks in places. What appears to be solid ice isn't because it's weakened by all the vegetation. Right now it's too easy for someone to get stuck. And with all the overgrowth, you can't see someone if they're in there. I ran out there this morning on intuition. I couldn't see that boy in the pond from the house. I couldn't even see the broken grass or cattails where he'd gone in either. I didn't see anything until I was right there in front of it. If Gus hadn't been barking, and the boy hadn't left his bike lying by the side of the house…if I hadn't gotten that feeling something was wrong…" She shuddered.

"What exactly needs to be done to restore the pond and make it safe?" Kat asked. "Is this something a few days with a backhoe could accomplish?"

"I think it's more complicated than that," Daisy said. "She probably needs the silt removed as well as some of the plants, but I think there's planning and knowledge that goes into restoring a pond—planning and knowledge none of us have."

Suzette took another sip of her wine and thought. "I'd definitely want the pond dug out, the dock fixed, the grasses cleared up, and an aeration system put in. And a fence," she added.

"Maybe you should get an estimate," Violet suggested. "What if it's not as much as you're thinking? What if you could do it in stages?"

"Violet's got a point," I said. "If it would make you feel better to fence the pond in until you got the money together to restore it, we could all help. It would probably be the crookedest fence line in the history of the county, but I can help dig post holes and nail boards."

"A lot of us can help, and we've got a few people in the neighborhood that might be willing to chip in supplies," Daisy said. "We could make it a block party. Cook food for everyone. Have beer—well, beer after we were done with the fence. Otherwise it really *would* be a crooked mess."

Suzette smiled. "I appreciate the offer. And I'll definitely consider it. As Kay said, it's good to have alternatives. Getting an official quote on a pond restoration instead of just having people tossing out numbers is a wonderful idea. And I'll look into the costs for fencing materials. But I still want that developer to come out and take a look at the property. He offered to have it surveyed at their cost so he could decide what sections of land they'd be interested in buying and how many houses they could put up there."

I caught Daisy's quick grimace, and barely hid one of my own. What Suzette did with her own property was her business, and it did seem hypocritical to be against additional houses when we were all benefiting from the development her family had done over a century ago. Still, I hated to see her lose more of her family's land, especially when I knew how much tradition and history meant to her. And in all honesty, I really didn't like the idea of half a dozen or more houses crammed into the end of the block where there was now a wide-open field.

"Maybe there's a grant or something you could look into to help with the pond restoration costs," Violet mused. "I'll bet there's something at the state-end for land preservation. I'm thinking you should contact the Locust Point Historical Society and ask."

"That's a great idea." Suzette smiled. "Thanks, ladies. Just talking this out with you all has made me feel so much better. Olive always is warning me against making hasty decisions, but I was so upset this morning that the only option I could see was selling off the land. If I could fence the pond and apply for grants…well, maybe I won't have to sell after all."

"Speaking of Olive, where is she?" Daisy asked.

"End of quarter." Suzette sighed. "She's determined to get everything done so she doesn't need to work this weekend. I'm hoping she'll be here before six, but it might be closer to seven."

A few more cars pulled up to the curb, and a familiar black SUV turned in our driveway. I couldn't help the smile curling up my lips. Judge Beck was home. And suddenly the world felt just a little bit brighter, as hokey as that might sound.

"What?" I turned as Suzette repeated my name.

"I was saying that it looks like you've got a lot of money in that donation bowl," she said. "And lots of sign-ups to deliver meals as well."

I glanced over at the bowl, thrilled at the generosity of my friends and neighbors. "I stopped by the hospital this afternoon and met with Travis's mom, Linda."

"How is Travis?" Suzette asked.

"They're keeping him sedated for now." I told the group what Linda had said and conveyed her gratitude to Suzette for what she'd done to save her son.

Suzette flushed. "I just hope I got there in time and that he wasn't under for too long."

"Me too," I replied. "I'm going to go in tomorrow and drop off gift cards. Did you want to come with me?"

"I think I'd rather wait a few days until Travis is out of the ICU, and conscious," she replied. "But check with me in the morning. I might change my mind. I just don't want Travis's mom to have to deal with a bunch of strangers crowding into the hospital at once."

"I'll swing by in the morning after yoga," I told her. "I'll even bring by a coffee cake or something for breakfast."

"Ooo, I'd love that." Suzette's expression brightened at the thought.

"Did someone say coffee cake?" The judge asked as he climbed the porch stairs to join us.

"Okay, I'll make two coffee cakes." I laughed.

"Good." He put his arms around me, holding me tight and planting a kiss on my cheek before releasing me to grab a beer and go greet the rest of our guests.

"You two are cute," Daisy teased.

And I couldn't help but agree. We *were* cute. I'd been happy to have the judge as a much-needed tenant, then been thrilled when we'd become friends. But now? Now, I couldn't imagine this house without him.

I couldn't imagine life without him.

CHAPTER 6

The next morning I was up an hour before Daisy was due to come over for our morning yoga. The house was silent except for Taco, purring as he wove in between my legs. I fed my cat, put on a pot of coffee, then decided to cook a big breakfast—biscuits and sausage gravy.

While the sausage was browning in the pan, I mixed up the dough, deciding to do drop biscuits. With them in the oven and the sausage still cooking, I got out my recipe box, deciding I'd make the two coffee cakes later this morning, after yoga and breakfast.

I let the sausage cook until it was dark brown, chopping it into small chunks with a wooden spatula. Pulling the biscuits out of the oven, I set them aside, then grabbed the spices, flour and milk to make the gravy. By the time Daisy arrived, the rich peppery smell of the sausage gravy had filled the air, mixing with the aroma of coffee and biscuits in a mouth-watering combo.

"Oh wow," Daisy eyed the sausage gravy as she poured herself a mug of coffee. "Are we eating breakfast first? That smells amazing."

"If I eat breakfast first, I'll never be able to do those yoga positions," I told her. "One downward dog and it's liable to come all up."

"Eww. Visual." Daisy laughed. "Then let's do our yoga first. Keep those biscuits and that sausage gravy warm."

"They'll be warm in my belly," A masculine voice teased.

I turned around to see Judge Beck with his messy morning hair, his Ninja Turtle pajama bottoms, and worn T-shirt. Pulling a mug out of the cabinet, I poured him a coffee and handed it over.

"Don't eat all the biscuits and gravy," I warned him. "And can you give it an occasional stir while Daisy and I do our yoga, please?" It wouldn't be the end of the world if we came in to gravy with a film on top from sitting on the stove, but since the judge was here, I figured I'd ask him to keep an eye on the breakfast.

"I can wait to eat until you all are done." He smiled.

"No, go ahead," I pulled out a plate and handed it to him. "You can always have more when we're back in."

He laughed. "Trying to fatten me up with second breakfast?"

"Trying to give you incentive to stay in the kitchen and stir the gravy," I countered.

He put two biscuits on the plate, and was spooning the sausage gravy on top as Daisy and I went into the backyard. Lady was already there, doing zoomies around the fence line. She saw us, and with a happy yip ran up to dance back and forth in front of Daisy.

"Oh, all right." Daisy dug in her jacket pocket and pulled out a palm-sized plastic frog. She gave it a squeak, and handed it over to Lady, who snatched it from her hand and began racing around the yard, stopping occasionally to toss the frog into the air and catch it.

"It's her favorite toy," Daisy told me as we spread out our

mats. "Sadly, when it comes to Mr. Frog, Lady's love is deadly. She's been through three of them in the past week. I'm now buying them in bulk, and hiding them, not letting her play with them except a few hours each day. The dog is obsessed. I think she loves that toy more than her food—and for Lady, that's saying a lot."

The dog continued to run around, occupied with her toy while Daisy and I rolled out our mats and began our yoga. Unusually silent, we practiced with only the occasional sounds of Mr. Frog squeaking. As we finished and were folding up our mats, a few stray flakes of snow began to come down.

"We finished just in time," Daisy commented.

Yoga with snowfall sounded idyllic, but in reality it was cold this morning, and I was grateful to be heading in to coffee and a hot breakfast. I'd rather enjoy the spring snow from the window than be trying to do planks on a wet mat.

The judge was happy to have a second plate of biscuits and gravy and keep Daisy and me company as we ate. Taco went from person to person, insisting that no one had fed him breakfast while Lady curled up on a towel by the door, watching Daisy with rapt attention.

"It's my turn to share gossip," I told the judge and Daisy after taking a few bites of my breakfast. "Miles told me that Peony might be released early—as early as next month."

Daisy sucked in a breath. "Ooo, Violet must be so excited. I wonder if Madison knows yet?"

"She hasn't said anything," Judge Beck replied.

Peony was one of Madison's friends, and the judge had never been particularly thrilled about that. Honestly, I thought Madison was a good influence on the girl, and hoped they'd continue to be friends. Peony would need all the allies she could get in this town.

"I don't know what she'll do about school," I said. "Maybe she'll finish out the school year and graduate next year, or maybe she'll decide to take her GED. Either way, I'm sure she'll need some sort of job to satisfy her parole."

"It's not going to be easy for her to find a job," Daisy said, echoing my earlier fears. "I could bring her on as a volunteer at work though. Or I could put in a word for her at the animal shelter. They're always looking for volunteer kennel techs, and I know they'll be willing to bring her on in spite of her record."

"It would be great if she had some volunteer options. I was going to talk to Matt as well and see if she could help out with some of his fundraisers," I mused. "I'll put together a list and give it to Violet. Miles said Peony is most likely going to live with her after her release."

"I'll bet Miles loves that," Judge Beck drawled.

"Well, he's going to have to learn to love that, since Peony is his fiancé's sister," I shot back.

The judge held up his hands in defense. "I know, I know. I'm just saying it's not an optimal way to start your marriage, having your sister-in-law living with you."

"There's a chance Peony may be out on her own before the actual wedding," I told him. "Miles said Violet has tentatively picked next June. As in not this June, but next year's June. That'll give Peony over a year to get settled."

"And if not, then they'll just need to get a bigger apartment to accommodate the three of them plus Hutch." Daisy laughed at the judge's expression. "One big happy family. Maybe a few of Violet's other sisters will move in as well. Or maybe her mother."

"Poor Miles." Judge Beck chuckled. "Hopefully love conquers all, even interesting in-laws."

Daisy ate her last bite of biscuits and gravy, and rose to

put her plate in the dishwasher. "Speaking of love, I know I'm a third wheel here this morning. I'll get out of your hair so you two can do whatever you do on a lazy weekend when the kids aren't here."

I felt my face heat up at the thought. The judge and I had been taking things slow, but we were grown adults, and our alone time had begun to include a few steamy interludes—interludes that vanished in favor of PG-rated affection once the kids were in residence.

I saw Daisy and Lady to the door, then headed back to the kitchen to find Judge Beck was finishing up the dishes and was putting the leftovers away.

"So what naughty things are we old-timers going to get into this morning?" he teased. "Reading the news? Mopping the kitchen floor? Bundling up and cuddling on the front porch as we watch the snow fall?"

"Baking coffee cakes," I told him, although the cuddling-on-the-porch idea sounded good. Much better than the other two options. I mean, mopping the kitchen floor? How was that naughty? Unless we were doing it in our underwear, that is.

The judge stepped away from the sink, pulling me in for a quick kiss that had me rethinking my morning plans.

"You get to baking. I'll go grab my shower," he murmured as he broke the kiss.

I clung to him for a few seconds, just enjoying having him close. The warmth of his skin, the softness of his pajamas, the brush of his raspy whiskers on my face. There was something so comforting about love. Yes, there was desire stirred into that mix, but the feelings churning their way through my heart were so much more than just physical in nature.

I'd had love once. How could I be so blessed to experience it a second time in my life?

Stepping back, I watched the judge head out of the

kitchen, then with a happy sigh, I got to baking. Once the coffee cakes were in the oven, I went upstairs to grab a quick shower of my own, coming back down just as the buzzer went off.

"I might have to save this for lunch. I'm still full from the biscuits and gravy." Judge Beck said as I took the coffee cakes out of the oven.

"We can always wait until after dinner." I glanced over at him, noting that he was wearing jeans as well as a T-shirt that was a whole lot less worn than the ones he used to sleep in. "Did you have anything planned for the day? I'm going to take one of these over to Suzette's and visit a little. I probably won't be more than an hour or two."

"I've got errands I was planning on running today—an emissions test for the SUV, then I figured I'd get the oil changed and a car wash and vacuum since I'll be out. Did you want me to grab something for dinner? I was going to swing by the grocery store anyway and pick up food for the kids for this week."

I nodded. "That sounds great. I'll need to run ahead and buy those gift cards and go by the hospital to relieve Linda so she can go home for a shower and change."

I wrapped some foil around one of the hot coffee cakes, then pulled out a knife and hovered the blade over the other. "Taste test?" I asked the judge.

He grimaced and held his stomach. "I'll explode. Honestly, I think that second helping of biscuits and gravy wasn't the best decision. It was so good that I couldn't help myself, but now I feel like I've gone up a few pant sizes."

I laughed. "Well, you still look good to me. We'll have this later." I wrapped up the second coffee cake and set it aside on the stovetop to cool.

"Romantic dinner, then coffee cake for dessert?" he asked.

This time I went to him, wrapping my arms around his

waist. "It's a plan. And if you're lucky, we'll mop the kitchen floor in our underwear later."

"Half-naked housework?" He wiggled his eyebrows. "You, my dear, definitely know the way to a man's heart."

I laughed and held him tight, thinking that he definitely knew the way to *my* heart. Definitely.

CHAPTER 7

There was a car parked beside Suzette's in her driveway, and it wasn't hers or Olive's. Glancing at the blue Mazda as I walked by, I wondered who was here and if I was intruding.

But I decided that no one who came bearing a coffee cake was truly intruding. If Suzette was busy with her guests, I could just leave it and go. Besides, she knew I was coming. It wasn't like I was showing up unexpected and empty-handed.

Suzette answered the door, and I quickly realized that my presence was absolutely welcome.

"Kay! Come in!" She greeted me with a strained smile and a stiff inclination of her head that had me gazing past her to where two women stood by the dining table.

The taller one looked to be about my age. She had short, silver hair and was wearing a tailored, gray A-line dress that came to just below her knees. Her only accessories were small gold hoops in her ears, a large black tote, and a pair of low-heeled pumps. The other woman looked to be in her late twenties and was wearing navy pants, a tan button-down shirt, and shoes that from my vantage point looked identical to the other woman's. The younger of the two had dark hair pulled back into a low ponytail, and a pair of glasses that she'd pushed up onto the top of her head.

I hesitated for a second, thinking they might be from one of the local churches, here to invite Suzette to Sunday service, or to give her pamphlets and pray for her soul. I occasionally attended services at my church, and considered myself moderately spiritual, but I had never been a fan of the door-to-door method of Christianity. I'll admit I always hid when these people came to my house, and I was a bit surprised to see that they'd somehow managed to convince Suzette to let them inside.

"Come in!" Suzette repeated, taking my arm and practically yanking me through the doorway.

I held the cake pan tight, not wanting to drop it, and stumbled into her house. She closed the door behind me, sealing off my exit and trapping me inside with her and the two women. There were lots of ways I'd planned to spend my Saturday and listening to people lecture me about the status of my soul wasn't one of them. But Suzette was a friend, and that friendship extended beyond the occasional baked good offering, assistance, and companionship. Evidently friendship now included enduring being prayed over by complete strangers.

"Ooo, what did you make?" Suzette asked, as if she had no idea what I was carrying.

"Coffee cake." I extended the pan, having the cowardly urge to drop it and run.

"Wonderful! I've got a fresh pot of coffee on." She took the cake from me and turned to the other two women. "I'm so sorry, but I had plans with my friend, Kay, this morning. Maybe we can continue this discussion later?"

"Yes. We have plans," I repeated, trying to back Suzette up.

"This really won't take much longer," the taller woman said.

Suzette sighed. "Kay, these two ladies are with the Locust Point Historical Society. They came by to talk to me about grant applications and the historic nature of the property."

Oh. So not church ladies then. Although from my past experience, those on the board of the Historical Society were just as evangelical as people going door-to-door with Bibles and pamphlets.

"This property is an important part of the history of Locust Point," the taller woman lectured. "So much of our town's history has already been lost to new housing. The entire Miller property has vanished to development. This is the only house left from the founding of Locust Point. It would be criminal to have the rest of such a landmark property chipped away and turned into new homes."

Good grief. I glanced over at Suzette and made a face, thinking that I'd rather have people lecturing me about God and praying over my soul than this.

The younger woman shot her co-worker an exasperated look, then slid a stack of papers across the table. "So many owners of properties on the historical register find it difficult to comply with the regulations and the expenses an older home and property can bring. There are grants you can apply for. And while some of them may take several months for approval, it's a good alternative to pursue before you think about selling."

"The Hostenfelder family was one of the first settlers in Locust Point. This house was built in 1736," the older woman reminded us.

"I'm not planning on selling the house," Suzette shot back. "And I haven't decided anything yet. I'm glad you both came by, and thank you for the grant applications. I appreciate your taking the time out of your weekend to bring them over, but now that my friend is here, I really need for you to leave."

The older woman made a huff noise, picked up her tote, and headed for the door, shutting it firmly on her way out. The younger woman straightened some of the papers on the table, glanced at the door, then smiled apologetically at Suzette.

"Sorry. She's a little…intense. If you have any questions about the applications, please feel free to call me. And I'm happy to come out here on my own and look around. I can take notes of key features of the property that might help you better secure a grant. Plus, if I find something on a dig, like old pottery shards, that might also help with the grant. You'd be surprised what sort of artifacts are on old farmland like this, and developers aren't all that careful when they're excavating. A lot of history gets lost because we don't have a chance to find it before a bulldozer runs it over."

With another smile, she scurried after the older woman, shutting the front door quietly behind her.

Suzette sank into one of the dining room chairs. "I could use a slice of that coffee cake, if you don't mind. Actually, I could probably eat the whole thing right now, I'm so stressed. When I called the Locust Point Historical Society last night and left a message on their machine, I hardly expected them to come running over here on a Saturday morning."

I topped off Suzette's coffee and poured myself one before pulling out two plates and forks from the cabinet. "I know you don't need me adding to your stress, but they do have a point, even if their delivery was a bit heavy-handed. There could be some important historical artifacts on the farm. Maybe at least you should consider having them come out to survey or use metal detectors, or whatever they do to check, even if you end up deciding to sell to the builder."

"I know. I know." Suzette sighed. "I'd almost made up my mind up to sell the land yesterday, but I'm not so sure now. I should probably have one of those ladies look at the back three acres, and maybe try to get a grant or two before I decide. I still think selling off some of the property might be the best option, but I'm open to other ideas, and I'm not as inclined to rush on a decision as I was yesterday."

I slid a plate with a slice of coffee cake and a fork in front of Suzette, then sat across from her with a slice of my own. "Please don't feel like I'm pressuring you either way. It's your property. I just know how much you love this place with all the history of your family, and I hate to see you make a choice you'd regret later."

She nodded. "In some ways, it would be easier to sell. Instant cash. Less land to struggle to maintain. I mean, what am I going to do with that back three aces of field anyway? I'm not a farmer. It's not like I'm going to plant crops, and the development at the far edge of the field wouldn't be thrilled if I put a bunch of cows or goats in there."

"It would make a lovely orchard," I commented. "Although that probably would be just as much work as putting in corn or wheat or something."

Suzette tilted her head. "You know, that's actually a good idea. There used to be an orchard back there, long before my grandparents' time. It would be wonderful to fill those acres with apple trees once more. And to restore the pond. And rebuild the dock. And fix the old chicken coop and the barn that's ready to collapse. And..." She shook her head.

I nodded sympathetically. "Money. I know."

"Money." She made a frustrated noise. "If I sell that back three acres, then I wouldn't have to fill out a dozen grant applications, and have to meet whatever conditions the grant specifies. I could just take the money and fix up the house as

I want, maybe even have enough to fix up the pond. Or I could just sell the parcel with the pond as well."

"It would be easier," I agreed. "Although selling the land with the pond would put someone's house right up against your backyard. I'm not sure you'd want that."

"True." She sighed again. "I keep telling myself that there's no shame in selling the land. My ancestors did the same. That's why you all have those Victorian houses down the street. But part of me worries that selling will be one step closer to losing my family heritage altogether. And to make things worse, that woman implied that since the property is on the historical registry, I might be prohibited from selling unless I petition the board or something."

"What!" I stared at Suzette in horror. "They can do that? They can just decide to register your property then keep you from selling it?"

She snorted. "They can keep me from doing certain types of improvements as it is. Not that I'd want to, but I can't replace the windows with standard-sized, vinyl trim ones. I can't put siding over the stone and log exterior. I have to have a certain type of fencing—which is something I just found out this morning."

"That's ridiculous," I argued. "The Steadmans half a block down can put up a chain link fence, but you can't?"

She shook her head. "Nope. Not unless I want to fight the Historical Society in court, and I don't have the money for that. I'm not sure if they'd prevail trying to block me from selling to the developer, but they wouldn't need to. I don't have the money to hire a lawyer and fight against them for the right to sell. Them just filing the suit would block me."

I took a few bites of my coffee cake and fumed, wishing that Judge Beck had come along to give some legal advice. "Maybe the developer could defend against the suit?" I suggested. "It seems like they really want the property. They might be willing to fight the Historical Society for it."

"Maybe. But that money has to come from somewhere. If they're going to court, then they're going to pay me less for the land. And it might not be worth the bother to them. Even if they reduce what they offer me, they still might not want to spend a few years fighting those people just for the right to put in a few houses."

"If they're planning six or eight houses, then it could be worth the battle," I told her. "Values are going up, and Locust Point has a reputation as a good place to live."

"We'll see what the developer says on Monday," Suzette said. "He offered to have the place surveyed at his own cost, so he can figure out how many houses he could put on the land and put together a proposal for me. I went ahead and agreed to that with the understanding that him surveying the property didn't obligate me in any way to sell it to him."

"There's no harm in getting a survey," I agreed. "In the meantime, we can figure out costs for fencing, and you can look over those grant applications. This isn't a decision you need to make right away."

She sighed. "I know. I've got no idea what that boy was doing out in my pond, but I shouldn't let that drive my decision-making process. It *was* a kind of catalyst, though. I've been frustrated trying to fix the place up, and the old pond has been a worry to me for a long time."

"If you won the lottery, what would you do?" I asked.

"Fix the house. Plumbing, electric, stonework, and everything. I'd have someone do landscaping out front. I'd completely restore the pond with a new dock and an aeration system, and buy a raft. I'd even put in a little sandy beach area by the dock. I'd fence in the property, maybe plant that orchard in the back three acres." She smiled. "And more. I've got a whole wish list, and I'd cross every item off."

"But you wouldn't sell," I pointed out.

Her smile faded. "I wouldn't sell. But I'm not winning the lottery. I can't wait forever, hoping a fortune drops in my lap."

I ate another bite of my coffee cake. "My advice is to see what the developer says, let that Historical Society lady nose around with a metal detector, and fill out a few of these grant applications. Then see where it all leads."

Suzette picked up the two business cards on top of the grant paperwork. "Miranda Cook and Ann Baker."

"Which one is which?" I asked.

"Ann was the older one who was threatening to sue me. Miranda was the less pushy, younger one—the one that offered to come out and dig around for artifacts."

I nodded. "Then call Miranda. And relax. There's no need to decide anything now. Gather all your information, sleep on it for a day or even a few weeks, talk to your friends and family, then figure out what you want to do."

She smiled, holding up her fork. "And what I want to do right now is have a second slice of this delicious coffee cake."

CHAPTER 8

Suzette had that second piece of coffee cake while we moved on to other, more cheerful topics of conversation. By the time Olive came by, she was back to her positive self. My job done, I headed back, happy that the snow had stopped with only a light dusting remaining on the grass and sidewalks. Once home, I swept the walk, then forced myself to do a few loads of laundry rather than succumb to the food-coma nap I desperately wanted.

We'd raised two hundred dollars from my porch happy hour donation bowl. I divided the money into a grocery store gift card, a gas station card, and one for a meal delivery service, thinking that Travis's mom might not have the time for grocery shopping or cooking right now. It took way too long for me to pick out an appropriate card, not wanting anything too personal or anything that referred to the recipient being sick. I finally found the perfect one and signed it from The Locust Point Community, then stuffed it into the envelope along with the gift cards.

That done, I headed to the hospital, giving a grateful

Linda the envelope and urged her to run home while I held down the fort here at the hospital.

"Take a shower and do whatever you need to do," I told her. "I've got no plans for this afternoon. I can stay here for as long as you like, so you can get things organized at home."

"Thanks." She ran a hand through her hair. "I desperately need a shower and a change of clothes. I won't be long. They're taking Travis off sedation soon, and I want to make sure I'm here when he wakes up."

"I'll call you if there's any change so you can hurry back," I assured her.

"I absolutely appreciate this, Kay," she said with a smile.

I sat down taking out my phone as she grabbed her purse and left, wishing I'd remembered to bring a book or at least a few of the files from work to occupy me in the waiting room. After going through all the magazines on the table, I knew more about the current scandals involving the British royal family than I'd ever wanted to, and found that I disagreed with the majority opinion on "who wore it best." Finally I resorted to playing "Candy Crush" on my phone. Thankfully it was an uneventful afternoon. I was glad Linda had taken some time to herself, and happy that there hadn't been any emergency while she'd been gone.

When Travis's mom arrived back in the waiting room, she looked refreshed. Her hair was back in that messy bun, but it was damp, and the curls escaping the scrunchie were shiny and clean. The shadows under her eyes seemed lighter, and her yoga pants and loose cotton shirt looked far more comfortable than the work attire she'd worn since Friday morning.

"No changes?" Were the first words out of her mouth.

"No changes—at least none that were significant enough for the staff to come and tell me," I told her as I stood.

"I feel so much better." She reached out to shake my hand,

then changed her mind, giving me a quick hug instead. "Thank you again."

"You're very welcome." I picked up my purse, shoving my phone back inside. "You'll text me with any updates? If you have time, that is."

"Oh, absolutely. And please tell Suzette again how grateful I am that she saved my son."

"I will. I know she's signed up for one day on the meal train, so you should be able to thank her in person hopefully soon. Why don't I swing by tomorrow and bring lunch? I can give you another break to go home to shower and change again."

"Oh, I'd love that." She smiled. "And hopefully Travis will be awake by tomorrow."

I felt a wave of relief just thinking about that. It was going to be okay. I just knew it was all going to be okay.

* * *

INSTEAD OF HEADING HOME, I drove to the VFW to meet with my friend and charity-fundraising guru, Matt Poffenberger. A retired Airforce Master Sergeant, Matt's passion was fundraising for charities including Standing Strong, which provided a hotline and suicide prevention programs for veterans. His events also benefited the volunteer fire department, at-risk youth programs, and local foodbanks.

Matt was right where I'd expected him to be, getting everything set up at the VFW for Saturday night bingo. The girls and I made it a habit to attend once every few months. One of us usually won at least one of the coveted baskets full of goodies that we all shared. I waved at Matt, then plopped my bag on a table so I could help him set up chairs as we talked.

"Are you here early for bingo?" he asked, loading four chairs under one of his arms. "It's beef stew night."

"We're not playing this week, but we'll be here next week." Because next Saturday was chicken pot pie night, and we all loved a good chicken pot pie. "I wanted to ask you a question about fundraising," I added.

His expression turned to one of excitement. "Yes, I definitely want your help getting sponsors for the golf tourney this fall, *and* in getting raffle items for this year's fire department carnival."

I'd already signed on to help with the golf tourney, but the fire department carnival was a new one. Matt was always looking for volunteers, and it was difficult to say no when these were important charities in our community that really needed the money.

"I'll help with both those." I grabbed two chairs and followed him to a nearby table. "But I wanted to ask you about helping me with a fundraiser of my own that I'd like to have this spring. Suzette's property is an icon of the town. Her family was one of the first three families to settle in the area, and hers is the only house left standing from that time in our town's history. She's struggling to maintain the house and property, and I really want to host something to help raise money for improvements and repairs."

Matt set the chairs up, then turned to face me as I did the same. "You'll need to have a project you're raising the money for as well as a cash goal. For nonprofit organizations like Stand Strong, you can run an event to benefit the general fund because people know exactly what services their money will be used for, but with something like this, people will want to know if the fundraiser is to put a new, historically-accurate roof on the house, or to replace the windows, keeping the original sizes and trim from the pre-Revolutionary War days. Donors need to know specifically what the fundraiser is supporting."

"It's primarily for the pond," I told him. "Fencing it in for safety as well as restoring it."

Matt folded his arms across his chest and frowned. "That's going to be a hard one. Unless there's something particularly historic about the pond, or Suzette has suffered some sort of tragedy, it's difficult to be successful on a fundraiser that's for general land maintenance and improvements—even if that land and house have historic significance."

"Drat." I straightened the chairs. "Well, it was worth a shot."

"Now, wait just a moment here." He held out his hands. "Don't go running off all discouraged. I might have an idea of how this could work, but it'll be a whole lot more effort on the organizers' part, and it would mean Suzette would need to forego some privacy."

"What are you thinking?" I asked, hoping that Matt might have a solution.

"Like a carnival, but not a carnival," he mused. "A sort of reenactment, maybe? Tours of the house with a guide who can speak to the history, the architecture, and the people who lived there centuries ago. You could even continue the event outside, where a guide would lead people on a tour of the neighborhood that was once part of the farm, the land that still is part of the farm, and around the pond. They can talk about what sort of crops the family grew, what livestock they had, what events led to them selling off the land that the other houses were developed on."

"Maybe we could have games for kids," I thought out loud. "Old-fashioned games like coin tosses, pick-up ducks, and a Big Six wheel."

"The VFW has a dunk tank you could borrow if you want

to," he added. "I'd suggest having politicians in it if you can, because everyone will pay a dollar to dunk one of the county commissioners. The high school band uses it during the fire department carnival, and the kids pay a fortune to dunk their teachers."

I nodded, thinking if I went that route, then maybe I'd put Madison and Henry in charge of the dunk tank.

"You and your friends could bake some old-fashioned muffins or something and sell them," he continued. "I *think* Suzette's property is still zoned as agriculture, which means she wouldn't need a permit to sell baked goods or things like honey and produce."

"Wow, I didn't know that." Matt was so amazing, and I was brimming with ideas for a fundraising event. Now, I only needed to convince Suzette. I was sure my friends would help with getting the word out as well as with the planning and organization. And maybe those overly enthusiastic ladies at the Locust Point Historical Society could pitch in as well. If it helped preserve the house and land, I might be able to convince them to host the tours, telling visitors all the interesting things about the farm, the house, and Suzette's family.

I headed home, full of hope that Travis would continue to improve and soon be out of the hospital, and that Suzette would find a way to fix up her pond without needed to sell off her land.

It was a wonderful day. And I was looking forward to a relaxing evening with Judge Beck—with or without household chores in our underwear.

CHAPTER 9

Sunday morning I was up with the sun, enjoying my morning a bit more than yesterday now that the weather had warmed slightly. Daisy and I had our usual chat post-yoga and ate coffee cake while the judge slept in unusually late.

Judge Beck and I had both chickened out on the partially-clothed mopping idea and instead had just curled up on the couch together to watch movies after dinner last night. We'd each staggered off to our own beds later than usual, but still, it wasn't typical for him to sleep in like this.

He came down just as Daisy was leaving, grabbed a cup of coffee, then plopped down at the dining room table in his pajamas, nose down in a stack of legal papers with his laptop open before him. Thinking he'd probably had some emergency with work, I fed Taco, showered and dressed, and came down to find him in pretty much the same exact position as before, with only a slight change in the size of each stack of papers.

There was something about his rumpled dark blond hair,

scruff of beard on his chin, and those darned pajamas that made my heart go soft. Picking up his coffee cup, I refilled it and also brought him a slice of coffee cake on a small plate.

He glanced up at me as I set the plate down, the confused expression on his face letting me know that he'd been so engrossed in his work that he hadn't even noticed me picking up the coffee cup. That sort of thing might bother some women, but I loved it. I loved that he was dedicated to his job, that his role in the justice system was something he took so seriously. Eli had been a surgeon and just as dedicated. I guess this sort of man was my ideal.

"Sorry." He grimaced. "Thanks for the coffee refill and the breakfast. I thought this could wait for Monday, but I got a text late last night and need to look over these case files today."

I perched on the edge of the table. "Doesn't your paralegal do most of this research for you?"

I'd met Deanna several times, and appreciated her quick mind and cheerful attitude. Thinking of her made me realize I'd never thought to invite her to the porch happy hours. I should ask the judge to extend an invitation to her and her family—if he felt comfortable having an employee see him at home, in a relaxed wine-drinking atmosphere, that was. Lots of bosses didn't want to cross that line, and Judge Beck was a very private person. Although he seemed to be loosening up on having such a distinct line between professional and private life since moving in here with me.

"Yes she does usually do this research for me, but Deanna has a husband and two young children at home, and I really don't want to ruin any plans she might have for this weekend." He leaned back in his chair and sighed. "When Madison and Henry were young, I spent every weekend working. I don't want Deanna to do that. And I know that if I ask her she'd do it. Even if I give her the option to say no, she won't say no. So I'll do this myself instead."

And with that, my heart just melted even more.

"Was there something you wanted to do today?" he asked. "I could take a break later this afternoon. I jumped right into this, since I wanted to get it all done before the kids came over."

He and Heather exchanged the children on Sundays, and the judge was determined to correct the mistakes he felt he'd made as a parent when they were young. When Madison and Henry were here, he put them first. He was up when they were getting ready for school, and was flexible about picking them up from various sporting practices. He rearranged his schedule so he could go to their games and volunteer at school functions. He made sure we all sat down for dinner together each night, and only went back to his laptop when the kids were busy on their schoolwork.

I could tell from the worried line between his eyebrows that he thought he was neglecting our still-early relationship, that working on a Sunday morning when I might have expected us to go somewhere or spend the day together, would cause a rift between us. That wasn't the case at all. Neither of us were young anymore. He had commitments. I did as well.

"Actually I was going to go over to the hospital to bring Linda some lunch and check to see how Travis was doing," I told him. "I might be back around one or two, but it could be closer to four if Linda wants to run home again and take a shower. While Travis is unconscious, she doesn't really want to leave without someone being there."

The judge nodded, relief flickering across his expression. "Then I'll just work, and get things ready for Taco's party tonight."

Oh, Lord. I'd almost forgotten about my cat's gotcha day

party. What kind of horrible cat-mom would do such a thing?

"I'm sure the kids will want to help with party prep, so don't do too much," I told him. "I'll be home before Heather drops them off—or right around that time."

"Sounds good." He gave me a distracted smile, his gaze already straying back to the stacks of papers.

I rumpled his hair, leaning over to give him a quick kiss on the cheek before grabbing my coat and hat, and heading out.

There had been many days after Eli's accident ten years ago when I'd paced the hospital floors, eating food from the cafeteria and vending machines, and sponging myself off with paper towels and hand soap in the hospital bathrooms. Those had been dark days, and I remembered the things I'd needed and appreciated when all my attention had been on my husband's health. So I decided to put together a little gift bag for Linda.

Stopping by a store, I grabbed one of those crescent shaped neck pillows, a package of wet-wipes and some travel-sized toiletries along with a small makeup bag to put them in. To that I added an assortment of magazines, a paperback novel, a small notepad and a few pens, then some mini candy bars, peanut butter crackers, and a package of trail mix.

Throwing it all into a gift bag, I headed over to the deli where I got a turkey and pepper jack on wheat as well as a Rueben, thinking I'd eat whichever one Linda didn't choose.

There were some closer spots in the hospital lot today, so I grabbed one and hauled the gift bag inside, waving at the woman behind the front desk and heading straight to the ICU. Linda wasn't in the waiting room, so I asked for her at the nurse's desk, assuming she was back at Travis's bedside.

"Oh, she's upstairs," the nurse exclaimed. "Her son

regained consciousness late last night, and remained stable, so they moved him to a room."

"That's amazing news!" I'd hoped the Travis had come around, but was worried that it might take a few more days. I realized I'd been drawing parallels between the boy's condition and Eli's right after his accident. I'd been almost afraid to expect anything about Travis—that somehow I'd jinx his recovery if I made any assumptions.

"Let me look up what room he's in." The nurse started typing on her computer. "I know his mother would really appreciate the visit, and Travis probably would as well. She hasn't left the hospital aside from that time yesterday when you relieved her to go home to shower. I don't think she's even called anyone except the boy's father."

"Has he been by to visit?" I asked, not sure what the situation was between Linda and her ex.

"I think she said he's supposed to arrive later today." The nurse wrote a number down on a piece of paper and handed it to me. "He's out in Oregon somewhere and had to do like five transfers to get here in any reasonable sort of time. Poor guy has been on a bus since Friday afternoon."

"Oh wow." I'd figured he would have jumped on a plane, but if Linda was struggling financially, I shouldn't have assumed her ex's situation would be better. I know if I'd had a family emergency on the West Coast, I would have been hard pressed to come up with the money to fly out myself.

I was willing to bet that Linda wasn't too happy about having to deal with her ex after not seeing him for so long, but from what I'd learned about the woman in these few short days, I knew she'd put on a smile and be polite for Travis's sake. His dad must care or he wouldn't have scrambled to get here via a convoluted bus route. And if the bus was his only affordable travel option, finances probably were the reason he hadn't see Travis regularly.

But in an emergency, he'd come. I hoped this would give him time to connect with his son and maybe repair some bridges. Judge Beck regretted all the times he'd missed when his kids were growing up. Travis's dad probably felt the same.

I thanked the nurse and headed up to the third floor, wandering the halls until I found room three-forty-three. The door was ajar, so I knocked softly, then poked my head in with a "hello."

"Kay? Come on in!" Linda's voice rang out with an almost manic excitement.

I went in and quickly saw why she was so happy. Travis wasn't just conscious, he was sitting up, awake *and* alert. There was a Styrofoam cup with a straw on the table in front of him. The monitors next to him beeped rhythmically. There was an IV in his arm, and a nasal canula for oxygen just under his nose, but his color was good and his eyes bright.

"Are you the woman with the cabin and the pond?" Travis asked, his voice raspy and raw. He squinted at me, then shook his head and spoke again before I could respond. "No, you're the lady with one of the big Victorian houses. You've got a gray cat that I can see perched in the window seat when I bring your paper by."

"Yes." I smiled, thrilled that he knew who I was—or rather that he knew who my cat was. "I'm Kay Carerra. My friend Suzette is the lady with the cabin and the pond."

His expression sobered. "Please tell her how sorry I am that I was in her backyard. And thank her for saving me. The doctors, the nurses, and Mom all say if she hadn't found me, pulled me out of the water, and given me CPR, I'd probably be dead."

I shuddered. He was too young to be facing his potential

mortality, to be realizing how close he'd come to losing his life.

"Does someone have my bike?" He suddenly asked his mother. "I left my bike there. Did someone grab it and bring it home? I don't want to lose it."

"It's at Suzette's," I reassured him. "I'll have someone bring it by once you're released from the hospital."

Teenagers. He'd almost died, and he was worried about his bike. Although I couldn't really fault him for wanting to make sure he got it back. He used the bike for his paper route, and probably his transportation to and from his job at the arcade. He wouldn't be using it in the next few days, but kids seemed to bounce back so fast. He probably figured he'd be back to delivering papers by the next week.

Even looking at him with the monitors and IV line, it was hard to believe he'd come so close to death just two days ago. My mind returned to him on that stretcher, the paramedics hovering over him, a ghost nearby that for a few seconds I'd thought was his spirit.

The memory made me blurt out the question that had been on all of our minds since Friday even though I probably should have waited.

"Why did you go back there? And go into the pond?" I asked.

His face reddened and he looked at the table in front of him, reaching out to fiddle with the straw in the cup. "I didn't mean to go into the pond. There were grasses and briars and it was muddy. With the ice and the little bit of snow, I thought I was still on the bank, then I fell through. I remember being surprised that it was over my head there, and the cold water took my breath away. I tried to swim up, but it was so cold none of my arms or legs seemed to work right. And I think I was tangled in some grasses or something. I don't remember anything else until I woke up in the hospital last night."

Linda had put her hands to her face as her son talked, turning away from him. I knew this was hard for her to hear. She'd known how close her son had come to dying, but hearing about his struggle, his last memories before he'd lost consciousness, were difficult for anyone to listen to, let alone the boy's mother.

"But what made you go behind Suzette's house and go into the briars and weeds around the pond?" I asked again.

"The drone," he told me.

"The what?" Linda and I both asked in unison.

Travis sighed. "Drone. I could hear it. I probably wouldn't have seen it in the dark but it had a little blinking light on the front. I saw the light and wondered what it was, so I pulled my bike over to watch. It was really low, only ten feet or so above the ground. Then something happened and it went down near the pond. I didn't see anyone around that could be piloting it, so I figured they were doing it from a couple of blocks away and that they might pay a nice reward to someone who found the drone and brought it back to them."

"Drone." I frowned. "Those giant spider looking things people fly around to take pictures and videos?"

He nodded. "Some of them have night vision cameras, and some have heat sensors, and others have metal detectors and X-rays. The high-end ones can do just about anything. The military has even got some that they use. They're cool. Well, not the military ones. I've never seen those. Actually, I've only seen the cheaper ones a few of my friends got for Christmas this year. Those are amazing, so I bet the expensive ones are *really* amazing."

I'll bet they were. But why was someone flying a drone around pre-dawn in a residential neighborhood?

"Where exactly was the drone flying before it went

down?" I asked. "Along the street? In people's backyards? Near parked cars?"

Call me suspicious, but I worried that a drone might be a useful tool for a robber trying to case a neighborhood, or a particular house, or even cars for a future criminal spree.

Travis shook his head. "No, it was going up and down that big unkept field behind the cabin. I watched it for a while because I was pretty much done with my paper deliveries and had some time before I had to be back home to get ready for school. It went up and down like in a grid pattern, then dropped low and started going slowly around the pond."

I frowned, wondering who was searching around Suzette's land—and why. There was being plain old nosy, and there was violating someone's privacy. This was the latter. Unless the owner of the drone hadn't known the field belonged to Suzette, that was. I hadn't known until Friday. If the drone owner thought it was just a big, unused, overgrown plot of land, then maybe they felt it would be an okay spot for some early-morning fun with a new toy.

"Did your friend find the drone?" Travis asked me.

"No, but we'll look for it." I waved a finger at him. "Not you. Not your friends."

The owner could have come and retrieved it themselves Friday while Suzette and the rest of us were at work. I'd definitely check with her though. If Suzette had found it and if I could somehow trace who it belonged to, I'd give that person a piece of my mind. I might even encourage Suzette to talk to the police, just in case the owner's motives weren't all so innocent. I wasn't sure if flying a drone over someone's private property was a criminal offense or not, but this whole thing creeped me out.

"Okay." Travis fiddled with the straw in his cup again. "It's not like I can go looking for it now anyway. I'm kinda bummed I won't be able to collect a reward, though."

"I'd rather have you alive than any darned reward," his mother shot back.

I agreed. And as much as I wanted to question Travis more, the boy looked exhausted. I felt guilty for wearing him out not even twenty-four hours after he'd been released from the ICU.

"I brought lunch," I told Linda, belatedly remembering that I was carrying the food. And a gift. "I also brought a few things I thought you might need. Although with Travis doing so much better, you might not need some of these items after all."

She took the bag, exclaiming with gratitude over the little items I'd picked up. Once she was done, I extended the bags with the sandwiches, thinking that I'd pick something else up for my own lunch now that Travis was awake and I wouldn't be hanging out in the ICU family lounge while Linda ran home to shower.

"A Reuben and a turkey with pepper jack." I pushed a sandwich bag into each of her hands. "I don't know if Travis can eat yet or not. If so, he can have one. If not, then maybe you can save one for later."

"Thank you so much." She beamed at me. "Actually Rick should be here soon. I'll bet he's going to be hungry."

"Dad's coming?" There was no hiding the excitement in Travis's voice. The exhaustion faded away and suddenly he looked ready to jump up and run a mile. "All the way from Oregon? He's coming to see me?"

Linda's smile didn't quite reach her eyes, but I was pretty sure it was convincing to her son. "Yes. As soon as I told him that you were in the hospital he got a bus ticket, and has been on the road since. I called him when you regained consciousness, and he's so relieved. He should be here in a few hours."

"Then I'll get out of your hair so you can spend some one-on-one time together, and spend some family time once Travis's dad gets here." I nodded at Travis. "I'm glad to see you awake and alert."

"Come back and visit." He grinned at me. "And let me know if you find that drone."

CHAPTER 10

I stopped by the Cozy Diner for a solo lunch, did a little bit of window shopping downtown, then headed home. At the last moment, I changed my mind, driving past my house and swinging by Suzette's. Her car was in the driveway so I pulled in for a visit, telling her the good news about Travis while she poured us each a cup of coffee.

"He's awake?" Suzette's eyes widened.

"Awake and alert," I told her. "He was sitting up and talking, although he did look a little tired after we spoke."

"Maybe I'll run over tonight to visit," she said. "I'd been holding off, wanting to wait until he was out of the ICU before I went over."

"His dad is coming into town, so I think it might be a better idea to at least wait until tomorrow," I cautioned. "From what I've been told, Travis hasn't seen his dad in a long time, so I think this might be an emotional reunion."

"Oh, in that case I definitely don't want to disturb them. I'll wait until he's home from the hospital before I plan a visit then," she said. "You have no idea how relieved I am to hear this news. I'll definitely sleep better tonight knowing he's on the road to recovery."

"Me too." I took a sip of my coffee. "He said the reason he was by the pond was because there was a drone flying over your property early that morning, and he saw it go down. He was over there looking for it, and didn't realize he was on thin ice near a deep part of the pond."

Suzette frowned. "A drone? Why would someone be flying a drone over my property? It's nothing but weeds and briars back there. It's not exactly picturesque. And why would they do it so early in the morning? It was dark out."

I nodded. "Travis said some of them have night cameras or infrared stuff or something. That still doesn't explain the why or the who."

She shook her head. "Great. Now I've got someone's drone in the pond. Well, *I'm* not going in there for it. If they want it back, they can pay to have my pond dredged for it."

"I was half tempted to throw on a pair of hip waders and go looking for it myself," I teased.

She laughed. "Do you even have hip waders?"

"No, but I'm sure J.T. does. He likes to go fishing," I added.

Suzette shook her head. "I think he fishes from a boat. I can't see J.T. standing thigh-deep in a stream for hours trying to catch fish."

"It might be worth buying a pair. Travis said some of these drones are expensive. He was hoping the owner would give him a reward for finding it." I absolutely wasn't going to go buying hip waders or trying to wander through Suzette's weed-choked pond, but it was a funny thought.

"I doubt they'd come forward to claim it," Suzette said. "They'd probably be too embarrassed to admit it was theirs. Whoever was nosing around my back property in the dark with a flying robot would have a whole lot of explaining to do. Isn't that trespassing? Isn't that illegal or something?"

I shrugged. "I don't know. It could be that they just thought it was an abandoned lot and not part of your property. I'll ask the judge though, or Miles tomorrow morning when he comes by the office. I'm guessing it's probably the sort of thing where they'd give someone a warning. Like if someone was trespassing by cutting across your backyard and you caught them."

Suzette leaned against the counter, cradling her coffee cup in her hand. "This really reinforces my belief that I need to do something about this property. I either need to find the money to fix it up, or sell the land I can't use. It's crazy to think that someone was flying a drone around that field and near the pond, and that Travis almost died trying to retrieve it. What's next? People dumping garbage under the light of the moon in the back field? Teens sneaking there to party? With all the weeds and brush grown up, I probably wouldn't even see or hear them."

Remembering the fundraising idea Matt and I discussed, I spoke up. "I might have an idea on how you can raise some money. Let me think about it a bit before I pitch it to you though."

"Well, I'm all ears," Suzette replied. "I'll consider any ideas at this point."

I stood and walked over to the kitchen window, looking out at the light dusting of snow that remained here and there over the brown grass. Patches of purple crocuses had burst into bloom, and I beside them could see the vibrant green that would soon bring forth daffodils. Maybe we *could* have the history tour Matt had suggested. The entrance fee would go toward pond restoration. People could sponsor an apple tree in the proposed orchard. Perhaps we could do some sort of Friends of the Hostenfelders club where we sent out newsletters with historical stories of the farm along with renovation updates for an annual donation.

A shadowy form caught my eye over by the pond. I watched as the ghost hovered near the spot where Travis had been found, then moved over near a patch of briars.

"Do you have ghosts here?" I asked Suzette, even though I could clearly see a ghost right by the pond.

"Oh sure. Not that I can see any of them, but sometimes I find a book or a picture that's been moved, or knocked over" She came to stand next to me. "Olive has been able to communicate with a few of them. There's one man who is very concerned about his crop harvest from 1793. Then there's a woman who lost three children in one month to smallpox. She likes to sit in the rocker in the loft bedroom that used to be the nursery and sing." Suzette pointed out the window. "There's a man who lingers around the pond and the old dock. He died in a battle during the Civil War and seems obsessed with the geese."

"Geese?" I'd never seen any geese in Suzette's pond, although I assumed at one time wild geese might have rested there during their migrations.

Suzette nodded. "Ages ago we used to have ducks and geese. There was a nesting box at the edge of the pond that's been gone since before my grandfather was born. My family used to raise them and butcher them for sale. From what I've read in old letters and diaries, it was especially lucrative around Christmas."

That made sense. I watched as the ghost made his way around the pond, vanishing over near where the dilapidated dock still rested, then appearing again across the other side of the pond.

"I wonder why a Civil War soldier is so interested in geese that he's been haunting the pond for around a hundred and fifty years," I mused.

Suzette shrugged. "Heck if I know. Olive says sometimes ghosts get stuck in a loop, repeating an everyday activity they once found comforting. It's not always an emotional or traumatic moment that roots them here. Occasionally it's something mundane, something soothing. I think if I died in battle far from home, I might want to spend all eternity walking around a pond and tending geese. That would probably be the very thing I was longing for at the time of my death, the thing I desperately wanted to return to."

I watched the shadowy figure make his loop once more, completely understanding that sentiment. I hoped the ghost's geese brought him some sort of peace, and that maybe one day, this soldier would be able to move on and truly be at rest.

When I saw Heather's car parked at the curb, I couldn't help but smile. Madison and Henry were here. Early. It was Judge Beck's week with the kids and I was so excited. Yes, having the kids in the house put a bit of a damper on our budding romance. They might know that their father and I were "dating," but neither the judge nor I were comfortable with public displays of affection around his children—well, affection that went beyond an arm around a waist or shoulder, or a quick peck on the cheek, that is.

I parked in the driveway beside the judge's SUV, then speed-walked across the lawn, practically skipping up the steps. Flinging open the front door, I found myself nearly flattened by a squirming, excited mess of brown fur.

"Cagney!" I knelt down and attempted to hug the pup while she painted my cheek with her slobbery tongue.

Heather had adopted the puppy at the urging of Madison and Henry, but over the last three weeks I'd seen how she struggled to adjust to Cagney's presence in her household as well as the care the young dog required. Judge

Beck had confided in me that he'd always wanted a dog when he and Heather had been together, and that she'd been the one who'd always nixed the idea, reasoning that he wasn't home enough to help take care of a pet, that the children were too young to help, and that she had enough to do without adding one additional four-legged responsibility.

I absolutely had supported her stance. As much as I cared about Judge Beck, he admitted he'd rarely been home during their marriage, and care for a dog would have fallen completely on Heather's shoulders. Things were different now, with the kids in their teens but it still wasn't easy adding a puppy to the family. I should know—I'd taken care of Cagney and three of her siblings for a week and had nearly lost my mind with the stress.

Well, the stress of puppies *and* the stress of solving a murder.

I stood, scratching Cagney behind the ears, and greeted Madison and Henry as well as Heather. Judge Beck stood behind them, a worried frown furrowing his eyebrows.

That wasn't good.

"Kay, can I talk to you?" Heather asked with a quick glance back at her ex-husband. "Alone?"

Definitely not good.

"Of course," I told her, because there really was no other response.

Heather walked past me out onto the porch and I followed, my stomach churning. Was this about the judge and me? Was I going to hear about how she disapproved of our romance? My thoughts spiraled downward, obsessing over the age gap between the judge and me, how I was supposed to be this grandmotherly figure opening up my home to him and the children, but that I'd suddenly become a cougar-y vamp, seducing her ex. Gritting my teeth, I stood in front of Heather, ready to withstand the storm of her scorn and disapproval.

Instead she burst into tears.

"I can't. I tried, but I can't, and that makes me a horrible person. I made a commitment. What does this say about the kind of mother I am, that I'm going back on my commitment after only three weeks?"

My eyes widened.

"I'm so ashamed," she added.

"I don't understand. Is there something wrong with Madison or Henry?" I asked, completely clueless about what had Heather so upset.

"Cagney." The word set off a fresh burst of tears. "I love her. I really love her. And the kids love her. But I always knew a dog was too much. Part of the reason I agreed to adopt her was because the kids wanted her. Part of it was me sticking it to Nate who'd always wanted a dog but didn't want any of the responsibility. Part of it was me thinking I'd be all alone when the kids went to college and it would be nice to have a pet to come home to."

"But it's too much," I finished for her. I totally understood. It was one of the reasons I'd adopted a cat at the shelter the day of Eli's funeral instead of a dog.

"The kids forget to walk her, or think a quick jog around the block is okay. And when they're here, I just feel overwhelmed."

I knew where this was going. And it wasn't like Judge Beck and I hadn't discussed the possibility that a puppy would be too much for Heather. She'd been reluctant, but had agreed because the kids wanted Cagney. And, as I had found out, it was very hard for a divorced parent to say no to the children they felt they'd crushed by the change in marital circumstances.

I put a hand on Heather's shoulder. "You've spent the last

sixteen years taking care of children and managing both a home and everything else for the entire family. I can't claim to know how that feels, but I did care for my disabled husband for ten years, and it was exhausting both physically and emotionally. When the kids are gone off to college, *then* think about getting a dog or a cat or a fish. Until then, maybe you just need to shift some of your focus to *you* instead of taking on another responsibility."

"I made a commitment," she sniffed. "I never thought I'd be someone who takes a dog home then brings them back to the shelter a few weeks later because it's hard."

"You're not bringing her back to the shelter," I countered. "We all decided on a month trial period. And I agreed that if it didn't work out, I'd give Cagney a home here."

She shook her head. "I feel like that's dumping the problem on you. You lost your husband a year ago. You're trying to find time for yourself as well. You've probably got less time for a puppy than I do, and Nate won't help at all."

Nate would most certainly help, or we were going to have words. But that was a conversation the two of us would have later.

"I knew there was a chance Cagney would be back, so don't feel bad about this. She has a home. She'll be loved and taken care of. Taco tolerates her. Actually, I think Taco secretly likes her, but he'd never admit that. There are four of us here every other week, and two the other weeks. And if we need a break, I'm sure Daisy would have Cagney over for a puppy playdate with Lady. I can get Molly or even Violet and Miles to puppy sit if we need. We've got more resources than you do. It'll be fine."

I patted her shoulder then stepped back as she wiped a finger under her eyes and sniffed again.

"Thank you. I still feel like a horrible person, but I realize this is best for Cagney. She'll be much happier here with everything going on as opposed to sitting in a crate all day at my house."

The crate. I grimaced. "She'll still be in a crate all day here. I can't take her to work, and neither can the judge. But she'll get lots of exercise and interaction in the mornings and in the evenings, and on the weekends."

Heather nodded. "I appreciate this, Kay. I really do. I brought by Cagney's crate, her bed, and all her toys and food, so you don't have to go out and buy anything."

"That's great." It was one less errand for me to squeeze in today before we got down to Taco's gotcha-day festivities.

I watched Heather leave, waving as she pulled away from the curb. Standing on the porch for a while, I contemplated how much my life had changed in twelve months. I'd become a widow facing dire financial circumstances. I'd adopted a cat and gotten a new job. I'd taken in a roommate, met two children I loved as if they were my own, and found unexpected romance. And now I had a dog.

The door opened and the judge came onto the porch, standing silently beside me and eyeing me with a questioning, somewhat apprehensive, look.

I let him stew for a few moments before speaking up. "So…I guess we now have a dog."

A grin split his face and he did a subtle fist pump he probably thought I couldn't see.

I turned to him. "And if you don't help me with her, I'm going to be upset. Very upset."

The grin widened. "Yes, ma'am. Can she sleep on my bed?"

I hadn't even slept in his bed. The dog was going to be in his bed before I ever made it there. The thought made me laugh.

"Yes, but I'm up before you so make sure you leave your bedroom door ajar so I can let her out to pee. I'll bring her outside for yoga." Daisy always brought Lady over, and I knew the terrier mix would be thrilled to have her old buddy back to play with while we did our morning exercise.

"Yes ma'am," he repeated. "Should I run over to the pet store? We'll need supplies."

I held up a hand to stop him. "Heather said she brought by everything Cagney will need."

His face fell.

"But I'm sure Cagney would love some new toys and treats, and maybe a collar with a tag that has our address and contact number on it," I added, remembering how thrilled he'd been to buy things for the puppies when we'd been fostering them.

He pulled a set of keys out of his pocket. "I'll be right back. Don't start the Taco festivities without me."

I shook my head, amused at his little-boy excitement over our new dog.

Judge Beck jogged over to his SUV, and I went back in the house, receiving the same greeting from Cagney that I'd just gotten not fifteen minutes ago. Dogs. It seemed any absence was too long where they were concerned. On the other hand, Taco was over by the couch, licking one of his paws and paying no attention at all to me. It would take some adjustment, having a dog in the house, but as I reached down and scratched Cagney behind the ears, I knew it was the right decision.

"Kids," I called out as I shut the front door. "It looks like we now have a dog."

CHAPTER 12

"Happy Gotcha Day toooo you!" We all sang as Taco ignored us. Every bit of the cat's attention was on the shredded chicken in his bowl.

Unlike Taco, Cagney was very interested in our song. She barked along to some of the words, ending in an aroooo bay that confirmed there was some hound in her checkered lineage.

We were eating tacos that Henry and Madison had prepared while their dad had gone off to buy half the pet store inventory. I'd never seen a man so excited before. It made me think that maybe Heather's returning Cagney was a blessing. He'd returned with toys, leashes, three collars, an assortment of chews and treats, and four bags each of different exotic dog foods, all of them promising to help our puppy grow into the sleek, powerful canine she was meant to be.

Taco had his chicken. Cagney had already eaten a bowl of dried kibble that Heather had dropped off because we weren't sure how her stomach would react to a sudden change in diet. Her leash was tied around the leg of the dining room table to keep her from trying to eat Taco's dinner. She'd been eying it since we put it in the bowl, and none of us wanted a cat-and-dog-fight to ruin the festivities.

Clearly we'd need to feed the two separately. Taco guarded his food with the ferocity of a tiger, and Cagney inhaled any edible item within reach as if she were a super-powered vacuum.

"Gift time," Madison called out as she pushed a stack of wrapped presents my way.

As Taco's primary human, I'd been designated the gift opener. The cat didn't have opposable thumbs, and was too busy with his chicken to care about packages. Although I was pretty sure the one oversized gift bag was going to become a cat toy regardless of what sort of present was inside.

The first gift was a battery-operated mouse toy with eyes that flashed red and a rope tail that swung around in a circle as the mouse raced around the floor. Henry volunteered to unpackage and assemble the toy while I moved on to the next package. That one held a crinkly cloth square stuffed with catnip, and a small hammock that Madison informed me should hang in the kitchen window so Taco had the perfect vantage point to watch the bird feeder in the back-yard. Another gift had fishy-smelling treats and a toy that looked like a burlap mouse had been genetically merged with a feather duster. The huge bag had an unassembled cat-tree with jute scratching posts, two comfy perches, and a fur-lined hidey hole.

My cat had made out like a bandit on his special day. And as predicted, as soon as he was done with the chicken, he went straight for the bag.

While Taco was scooting himself around the dining room inside a gift bag, the judge, the kids, and I assembled all the gifts. Cagney was especially interested in the mouse/feather duster toy, so I predicted that one would have a short life.

Maybe as short as one day from the intent, predatory expression on the pup's face.

After tempting Taco with all his new toys and ruining his vet-ordered diet with almost half a bag of fishy treats, the kids cleared the table, instructing me that I needed to remain seated.

I turned to Judge Beck, my eyebrows raised. He shrugged, trying to play it as if he didn't know what was going on, but that little smile he was trying unsuccessfully to hide gave him away. A few minutes later, the kids returned, singing once more. Henry was carrying a cake shaped like a cat with its back arched upward. I recognized right away that he'd used a Halloween cake mold, and had trimmed it a bit to make it look less seasonal. I was impressed.

Taco was a gray tabby, and Henry had tried to recreate his fur color with the icing. The white-vanilla stripes and chocolate stripes, I expected. But the gray… I didn't know what he'd used to create gray icing, and I wasn't sure I wanted to know. It didn't matter. I'd eat it regardless of what it tasted like, and I'd praise the cook to the heavens.

We finished singing and I leaned forward to cut us all slices—small slices, just in case.

"Henry made the cake all by himself," Madison announced.

I shot her a narrowed eyed glance, knowing that she wasn't complimenting her brother's cooking ability. No, Madison was washing her hands of the whole cake project, making it well known that if it was inedible, she'd had nothing to do with it.

We sat down, all of us staring at the cake and waiting for someone else to go first. The inside was golden pound-cake yellow; it was just that gray icing that had everyone hesitating.

I finally took the plunge, stabbing a chunk off with my

fork and sticking it in my mouth. I tried to swallow as quick as possible, but there was no way I could eat fast enough to avoid tasting the dessert.

Butter. Vanilla. A hint of chocolate. And…blueberry?

"This is really good," I told Henry with all honesty.

Because they'd clearly been waiting to see if I keeled over and died, or at least gagged, the judge and Madison finally took a bite.

"Did you use blueberries?" Madison asked, her tone somewhat accusatory.

"I did." Henry beamed. "Remember when Aunt Ida made that blueberry wine and everyone teased her because it wasn't blue or purple, it was gray? Well, I figured if I crushed some blueberries and strained the juice, I could add it to vanilla icing. It was hard because I didn't want to make the icing too runny, but I needed enough blueberry juice so it was actually gray."

"Just like Taco's fur." I glanced down at the cat who was once more in the giant gift bag, his tail and rump the only part of him visible.

"I can really taste the blueberry," the judge said. "It goes great with the vanilla and the pound cake. And the hint of dark chocolate icing is a great compliment. Good job, Henry."

"Yeah. Good job, Henry," Madison echoed with a little less enthusiasm.

She scarfed down her cake and went for seconds while I watched her. Madison had been eager to learn how to bake and cook and took great pride in her budding culinary skills. I knew her ego was a bit bruised that her little brother, who barely knew a spatula from a slotted spoon, had pulled off an amazing dessert.

"It's a box cake," Henry offered, as if he could sense his

sister's envy. "And I would never have known how to make the icing from scratch if Madison hadn't helped me."

The girl's expression brightened. "It's okay to start out with box cakes. And the blueberry idea was really brilliant. As is getting the icing the right color without it being all runny from the blueberry juice."

"Maybe you can help me make muffins this week, Henry," I said, knowing the boy's answer.

Henry's eyes widened. "I…uh…no thanks, Miss Kay. I…I, uh need to do some homework. For school. For Monday."

I hid a smile. He'd had fun making the cake, but Henry was not interested in baking as a regular hobby. Madison's position in my kitchen was safe, and the girl appeared relieved that her brother wouldn't be joining us in our baking endeavors.

"I do have some good news to share." I told them about my visit to the hospital and Travis' improved condition. We finished our dessert, then I said I'd do the dishes to give the judge some time alone with his children. Halfway through the cleanup, Madison came into the kitchen with an offer to help.

We worked in silence for a while. I didn't make small talk, thinking that there was something on the girl's mind that she needed to process before she got around to voicing it.

Finally Madison spoke, as she rinsed off the plate and handed it to me to load in the dishwasher. "I feel bad about Travis. I mean, I don't really know him that well or anything but I just feel gutted that a kid from my school almost died."

I remembered being her age. Death seemed like such a foreign concept—something that happened to the old and the very ill. When a boy in my high-school had lost his life in a car accident our senior year, I'd felt as if my whole world had been rocked.

Someone young had died. And if *he'd* died, then maybe I

could as well. That feeling of immortality I'd always had as a child had come crashing to the ground.

"I talked to some of his friends," she continued. "Travis's family doesn't have a lot of money. He's been doing that paper route since he was twelve, trying to save for a car and maybe college. Can you imagine that? He gets up at four thirty every morning to go out on his bike and deliver papers. And his friends said he also has an after-school job at the arcade."

"He sounds like a hardworking young man," I replied. It was good for Madison to realize that not everyone in her school had the same advantages she did. It was one thing to think of the homeless and those who couldn't put food on the table, but knowing kids that were less well-off than her family hopefully would make her appreciate all she had.

"It's not fair." Madison rested her hands in the sink and stared out the window to the backyard. "It's just not fair. He and his mother work so hard, and now…even if he gets out of the hospital totally okay, will they ever recover financially from this? If their insurance doesn't cover his stay, are they going to be facing huge medical bills? Will his mom lose her job because she had to take time off work to be with him? Will Travis lose the arcade job because he couldn't show up to work like he was supposed to?"

"So many people are one paycheck away from financial disaster," I softly told her. "Eli and I were doing very well financially—as well as your mom and dad. We bought this house and renovated it. We took vacations when he could get off work. I felt free to take risky assignments that might not result in a saleable story because we had a nice cushion. But then he had the accident, and that cushion was used up. We had good insurance, but it didn't cover everything. Our money ran out. Eli's disability payments ran out. We took on a second mortgage, went through our retirement and all of our savings. I refused to face it, but even with the social security disability payments, we were on the verge of having to sell the house and move within the year. Then when he died, I had to deal with additional medical and funeral expenses. If your father hadn't moved in, I'd probably have sold this house a month or two after the funeral and be in an apartment right now."

Madison's eyes widened. "Miss Kay! I had no idea. I just… I just didn't know."

I smiled. "Adults often hide a financial crisis from children, not wanting them to worry about something they have no ability to impact. I wish it was a rare occurrence, but it's not. That's why we need to take care of our neighbors and those in our community. There are government programs to help, and organizations and religious groups that can help, but we as individuals need to help as well."

She nodded, her jaw firm. "I started a collection at school, Miss Kay. I got approval from the principal and we have a round-it-up change jar in the cafeteria. Two of Travis's friends are taking over his paper route for him until he's able to resume work, and we did a petition to present to the arcade to hold his job for him. Ten of us went to the arcade on Saturday morning and delivered it to the manager."

I sucked in a breath, my heart swelling at how Madison had sprung into action, helping this student in her school that she hadn't even really known. "Oh honey, that's amazing."

"When this is over, I want to do more—for other kids in Locust Point that don't have the advantages I do. Maybe I can volunteer over the summer and after school. Mr. Matt knows all about raising money for charity, and Miss Daisy works with teens at her job, so I thought I could go to them, and get their thoughts on where I could best help."

"I'm so proud of you," I told her. "So, I guess you're not

going to push to go to Europe the summer of your senior year, then? If you're doing all this volunteer work, you might not have the time to take off. Unless this is just a one-year project?"

Her brow furrowed. "I want to go to Europe. I'd love to take a whole year and travel, but I know mom and dad would never go for that, so I'd thought about going the summer my senior year instead. But how could I travel to Europe when there are kids who can't even afford a used car to get to work, let alone college classes or a trade apprenticeship?"

"This is a good thing to volunteer, Madison, and I'm very proud of you." I took a breath. "But don't deny yourself any fun at all because there are those who are struggling. You're young, and you deserve to experience life. Maybe instead of a summer in Europe, you can take a week or two. Or do a semester abroad in college. Try to balance your desire to help others with a joyful exploration of what the world has to offer. You don't have to do the billionaire tour. If you keep things frugal on your trip and volunteer around that sched- ule, you can have fun and still keep true to your humani- tarian goals."

I was a bit worried the girl would bite off more than she could chew and burn out. Kids were so enthusiastic, and I knew they sometimes overcommitted themselves in wanting to help.

"Maybe you could start with something small," I added. "You've got several things going on to help Travis. I could definitely use your help on an activity I'm thinking about to raise money to restore Suzette's pond. And you could also help the committee that's organizing the Volunteer Fire Department Carnival. That'll give you some broad experi- ence in nonprofits and fundraising that you could use when you decide where to volunteer your senior year."

"That's a good idea." She reached out and hugged me.

"Thank you. When Mom and Dad split up, I was so angry and upset. I thought they'd ruined our family. But weirdly enough, things got better. Dad is happier. Mom is happier. And now we've got you and Taco and Cagney."

I hugged her close. "I love having you and Henry here as part of my family."

She peeked at me, biting back a smile. "And dad?"

There was no hiding my smile. "And your dad. We're all a family here. The whole bunch of us."

And now that family included Cagney.

CHAPTER 13

The judge, Madison, and Henry stood on my porch as I locked the front door. Cagney danced around by my feet, her leash in her mouth as if she were about to take herself on a walk.

Judge Beck had rounded his children up, insisting that if we were going to add a dog to our family then they both needed to take on responsibilities for her care. I hadn't been included in the lecture, but I'd put on my sneakers and coat to come along as well. We'd make this a family walk, because given our schedules, we probably wouldn't be able to do this together more than once or twice a week.

March meant sunset came sooner than anyone would have liked, but our block had enough streetlights to give a shadowy ambiance to the evening hour and cast enough light that none of us should be tripping over cracks in the sidewalks. Just in case, Judge Beck had grabbed a small flashlight off the hallway table and stuck it in his coat pocket.

We headed down the street, Cagney leading and straining at the end of the leash. The judge took over when he realized our puppy was on the verge of dislocating my shoulder. He pulled Cagney back with a few commands to "heel"—commands that she was trying very hard to ignore.

I sighed, thinking that I definitely needed to enroll Cagney in some obedience classes. I knew that Heather had done classes with the puppy, but clearly Cagney was the sort of dog that needed the extended training version and possibly some remedial classes.

"We need to discuss a schedule for taking Cagney on walks," Judge Beck said once he'd finally gotten the dog under some sort of control. "We can let her out into the backyard to go to the bathroom, but she's an active dog and needs to be taken for a long walk twice a day."

"I have to get to school in the morning," Madison said. "And softball practice is starting up on Tuesday."

"And I have Cross Country practice. And school as well," Henry added.

The judge turned a frosty glare on both kids that had them cringing.

"There are four of us," I said, giving Judge Beck and equally frosty glare. "If we divide it all up between everyone, then we can manage. I'll take tomorrow and do the morning as well as the evening walk. Who's up for Tuesday?"

Henry sighed. "I'll do Tuesday."

"And I'll take Wednesday," Madison chimed in. "We don't have practice on Wednesdays."

"Then I'll do Thursday," the judge offered.

We walked on in silence for a few moments, no one else jumping in to take Friday, Saturday, or Sunday. This was not going well. And things would be even more difficult next week when the kids were gone and the responsibility for Cagney would rest solely on the judge's and my shoulders.

"Friday is happy hour," I reminded the other three. "I'll take the morning walk, but I can't get everything set up for happy hour if I need to walk Cagney when I get home from work."

"Can she get enough exercise playing with the other dogs at happy hour? Or in the backyard?" Henry asked. "Just that one evening, and we can go back to walking her on Saturday."

"No." The judge's voice was firm. "She's going to be cooped up in the house all day while we're at school and work. She's a young dog and needs a walk twice a day."

"I'll do it Friday after school," Madison finally said.

"I'll do Saturday unless I have a cross-country meet," Henry said.

"There's no reason you can't walk the dog before and after your meet," his father scolded. "Just get up early, and take a flashlight if it's dark."

The boy sighed. "Okay. Then I'll do Saturday, and Madison can do Sunday."

"Perfect. Thank you both for helping out," the judge told them. We continued our walk, Cagney showing no signs of tiring. We passed Suzette's house, then turned at the end of the street to head back. The pup was still full of energy as we approached our house, so the judge decided to continue on for another few blocks in the other direction. The kids went with him, while I headed back inside.

The house felt eerily silent, the only noise the ticking of the mantle clock and Taco's happy chirp as he played with one of his new catnip toys. With the rare solitary moment, I decided to get started on my baking. Tomorrow was Monday and I not only wanted something ready for everyone's breakfast, but a special treat to take into the office. Kat's husband Will had Celiac disease, and she'd given me a gluten-free muffin recipe. I'd been wanting to try it out. Today was the perfect opportunity. If the muffins were horrible, I'd just swing by the bakery on my way in to work. If they were awesome, then I'd have one more muffin to add to the "favorite" tab in my recipe box.

I grabbed the two bananas off the counter that had started to turn black, then pulled the containers of coconut flour and almond meal out of the cabinet. The recipe called for maple syrup as a sweetener, as well as chocolate chips and walnuts. Everything went together in the mixer, and by the time the rest of the family had come back from the walk, I had muffins in the oven.

"Oh darn! I wanted to help make them." Madison sniffed as she came into the kitchen, then looked mournfully at the oven.

"It's a new recipe," I told her. "I only made a small batch, so maybe you can help me make something later this week."

"Okay, but I get to pick the recipe then," she said.

That meant we'd probably be making apple spice muffins, as they were Madison's favorite. Or those espresso chip scones she really loved.

I cleaned up in the kitchen while Madison and Henry headed upstairs. By the time the muffins were out of the oven and cooling, everyone had settled in to their nightly routine. Taco had abandoned his catnip toy and was sprawled on his new hammock, snoozing. Cagney was curled up in one of the many dog beds the judge had scattered throughout the house. Judge Beck was in the dining room, focused on whatever work he needed to get done for tomorrow morning.

I pulled one of the wrappers off a muffin, and took a tentative bite. They were still hot, so the chocolate chips were melty and steam rose from the center of the muffin. The texture was a bit more dense and moist than the muffins I'd made with wheat flour, but they were absolutely delicious. Thinking that they might be better cold, I threw half the batch into the fridge, deciding to taste-test once again tomorrow.

I'd solicit everyone's opinions on the new muffin recipe, but I was predicting these would be a hit.

With a final wipe of the counters, I grabbed my bag and went in to the dining room get a little work done. Around midnight, I bid Taco, Cagney, and the judge goodnight, then headed to bed, dreaming of muffins, apple orchards, and a Civil War soldier whose ghost haunted my friend's pond.

CHAPTER 14

Cagney left us a little gift in the hallway sometime during the night. I nearly stepped in it in the dim pre-dawn light, and had to run downstairs to get some cleaning supplies, dashing back to clean it all up before anyone else accidently walked through it. Thankfully it was a number-two and on the hardwood floor portion of the hall-way, so cleanup wasn't too difficult. Cagney came out of Judge Beck's room and stood in the hallway, her tail slowly wagging as she watched me on my hands and knees, washing the floor.

"This was my fault," I told her. "I'm the one who told Judge Beck to leave his bedroom door open. If you'd been closed in, maybe you would have been more inclined to wake him up and tell him you needed to go out, instead of pooping in the hallway."

Her tongue lolled out of her mouth and she tilted her head as she watched me. I got the feeling she might have just pooped in Judge Beck's room instead of the hallway, but then he would have needed to clean it up instead of me. How had Heather handled this? Had Cagney stayed in her crate all night? Or maybe she'd been fully housebroken, but the change in circumstances was messing up her digestive schedule?

I heard the front door open a split second after Cagney did, and shouted down the stairs, more worried that my dog would escape outside than me waking up the judge or the kids.

"Loose dog! Keep the door closed!"

"Sorry!" Daisy called up. "Cagney! Look how much you've grown, girl!"

I heard the jingle of more than one dog tag and knew immediately that Cagney and Lady were dashing around my house, happily greeting each other.

"I'm taking these two hooligans out back," Daisy said. "And putting on a pot of coffee."

Thank goodness, because I'd been too focused on cleaning up the mess in my hallway to think about coffee.

I finished up, then dashed out to the backyard where Daisy already had set up our yoga mats and Lady was doing laps around the fence line with Cagney tearing after her, little puppy legs pumping away as she tried to keep up with the older and faster terrier mix.

Daisy and I did our beginning Sun Salutations, our breath clouding in the frosty air. I was wearing an oversized sweat-shirt and long, thermal leggings, but I was still cold. The idea of another cold snap with more snow in the forecast made me shiver. And it made me think that the dunk tank Matt had suggested for the fundraiser at Suzette's would be a really bad idea.

"You're quiet this morning," Daisy commented as she led me into a series of planks and cobra poses where even thinking was difficult. "Is Travis on your mind?"

"Actually Suzette is on my mind," I told her with a grunt as we shifted into a Triangle pose.

As we twisted and turned, my core muscles burning, I told her about Matt's ideas and my desire to help Suzette pay for a fence and pond restoration without needing to sell the land or apply for grants.

"If she still wants to go for some grants to fix up the house or ends up deciding she wants to sell the land anyway, at least this will take the pressure of her need to make a decision," I gasped out.

"I think it's a great idea," Daisy replied, not the least bit breathless. "Count me in. I'll go to the neighbors to get glassware for the coin toss, and set up volunteers to run some of the games. I'll take care of the entrance tickets and keep track of the money as well."

"Thank. You." I said, as we lifted into a Warrior Two pose. "I'm thinking of hosting it in two weeks."

"That doesn't give us much time," Daisy commented. "We might raise more money if we could push it out until late April or even May."

I nodded, which went completely unnoticed since we were both currently in a Downward Dog position. "I know, but Suzette is upset and might not be able to wait another month or two on these repairs. I'm worried if we wait, she'll decide to sell before we even have the event."

"Good point." Daisy rose into a Mountain pose, and I followed, relieved to be finally standing up. "Why don't you talk to her and see? If she knows she'd be getting fundraiser money in a few months, maybe she'd be okay waiting before she decided to sell? I honestly think more people would want to come out and walk around her house and property when the weather is better."

Daisy had a point. We continued to talk about the fundraiser in between our yoga poses, then had a quick cup of coffee and a muffin afterward. After a quick taste test, Daisy and I both agreed that the muffins were best cold, so I put the rest of them into he fridge. Once Daisy had left, I ran up to grab a fast shower, knowing I needed to rush since today was my day to walk the dog.

The kids and Judge Beck were sitting at the kitchen island eating the banana, walnut, chocolate-chip muffins, and engrossed in the rush to ready themselves for school and work. I grabbed a go-cup of coffee, and clipped Cagney's leash on her collar, hoping a walk would wear her out enough that a day cooped up in a crate wouldn't be a hardship. I still felt uncertain about leaving her home all day in a crate. I realized that plenty of dogs were perfectly happy with that arrangement, and that as long as Cagney got plenty of exercise in the morning and the evening, she'd be fine, but I hated the thought of leaving her cooped up. I knew the damage a puppy could cause unsupervised in a big house, and that crating her was just as much for her own safety as that of my wood trim and furnishings, but I couldn't help feeling guilty.

Taco roamed free in the house all day, but he wasn't a puppy in the middle of a chewing phase. Daisy took Lady to work with her every day, but she also used a crate when she needed to go places where a dog wouldn't be welcome, like the grocery store. Besides, Cagney was comfortable in the crate. Heather had been crating her while she was at work, so this was the pup's routine.

Those were the things I kept telling myself as I walked the dog, trying to reassure myself that I was doing the right thing for Cagney.

She certainly was happy now, tongue out as she trotted ahead of me down the sidewalk. We went past Suzette's house, turned around and went past our house to the end of the block. Cagney was still going strong, so I decided to keep going, turning left and down a block to the row of houses whose backyards adjoined ours. As I got further down, the road veered to the right to loop around Suzette's plot of land. The houses here were more spaced out, with some of them having almost an acre of lush green grass of their own—well, lush green grass in the summer. Right now it was all a brownish color, some promising leaves of wan green poking through the crust of what remained of this past Wednesday's snow. As Cagney powered on, I peeked through the side yards to where Suzette's acreage stood—the unkept weeds of her property sharply delineated from the homeowners' clean-cut lawns. A few houses had fences, but many didn't.

Suzette's car hadn't been in her drive when we'd walked past. I hoped that she had opted to stay at Olive's place last night rather than go in to work early to make up the time she missed yesterday. As stressful as this weekend had been for her, maybe it would help if she had a night away from her own home.

The sound of raised voices caught my attention. I slowed then halted, Cagney straining at the leash in protest. Between the houses I could see an argument in progress between three men. The two on the opposite of the fence were scowling, hands on their hips, where the one this side of the fence gestured wildly, his voice raised. The most alarming part of all this was the man on my side of the fence was holding some sort of shotgun or rifle.

I honestly don't know if it was my investigative journalist past or present private investigator career that made me jump into what could have been a deadly situation. Most likely it was just my curiosity. Either way, I walked briskly between the two houses, Cagney in tow. When I was twenty or so feet from the man with the gun, I called out, not wanting to startle him.

"Hi! Is there a problem? I was walking by and couldn't help but hear you all arguing."

I kept my tone cheerful. All three men turned to look at

me, and I noticed the two on the other side of the fence seemed relieved by my presence.

"This old goat is threatening us." One man waved a hand at the one this side of the fence.

I grimaced. I was pretty sure his buddy grimaced as well. Complaining-man looked to be in his twenties, thin as a wire and wearing clothes that should have been a few sizes smaller. He had a utility belt around his waist holding a bunch of random tools. In one hand, he held what looked like a large tripod. His buddy was a stout man with his weight all in the front part of his stomach. He looked to be about my age, with lines in his deeply tanned face. He ran a hand over his bald head and eyed the weapon nervously.

"You're on my property," the man this side of the fence snapped. "I see someone climbing over my fence and messing with my land, and I'm going to assume you're a robber. Now get out of here. And don't come back."

My eyebrows shot up. Climbed his fence? I looked at the tripod thingie once more, wondering if the man was a private investigator taking pictures for a case. If so, he would have been better off apologizing and getting heck out of here instead of staying and arguing with the homeowner.

"I'm just doing my job," tripod-man snapped back. "And according to my paperwork, this fence isn't even on your property."

Whoa. I glanced back and forth between the three of them, my gaze settling on the homeowner. He was an elderly man—maybe in his eighties? Stoop-shouldered. Age spots clearly visible on his bald head from where I stood. A frame that had once held a physically strong man upright now had sagging skin and dwindling muscle tone. The hand that held the gun was firm and unwavering, and I hoped when I was his age, I still had such a steady hand.

Suddenly I realized the two men on the other side of the

fence were on Suzette's property, and the tripod was some sort of surveying equipment, not a photographer's tool.

"You're the developer," I said, looking at the portly man. "And you're a surveyor."

"Developer?" The man my side of the fence exploded, and the long gun was suddenly in a more shot-ready position. "You're not putting houses in my backyard. This is my land."

"It's not," the survey shouted. He put the tripod in the crook of his arm, then dug something out of his pocket. For second, all of us froze, me immediately thinking of options for cover for Cagney and I if this turned into some *High Noon* sort of conflict.

I'm pretty sure we all—well, all except for Cagney— breathed a sigh of relief when the survey pulled a paper out of his pocket and began unfolding it. Even the homeowner lowered his gun a few inches as he saw it wasn't a pistol.

"This is the land plot I picked up at the courthouse." The surveyor shook the paper at the homeowner. "It says this property extends ten feet past your fence line."

The homeowner's complexion turned an alarming shade of purple. "That's bull hockey! The plot I got when I bought this house fifty years ago says otherwise. The fence is actually offset two feet back from my property line. And if you say otherwise, I'll see you in court. Or at the business end of my shotgun."

"Whoa, whoa." I held up both hands, not sure how this was going to turn out. "I live a block over in a house that was built about a hundred and fifty years ago. My husband and I did some extensive renovations, and I know what a pain it is to dig up old survey and land records. There's probably just a mistake that occurred during a survey a hundred or more years ago, that can be easily resolved with some research at the courthouse. There's no need to threaten anyone, or be upset about this. Errors happen, especially back when everything was handwritten and it was easy to mistake a three for an eight or something like that."

The homeowner frowned, eyeing me more carefully and lowering the shotgun. "You're that investigative woman. The one who found out our mayor was a murderer. The one who caught that hussy who killed the football star."

I winced, wondering if Peony would ever escape the notoriety of being the "hussy" who'd killed Holt Dupree.

"Let me do some digging around," I offered. "I'll find out where the property line truly is. And if there was some error, and you inadvertently put your fence up a little over the line, then I'll put you in touch with the owner, Suzette Hostenfelder. She's a very nice woman, and I'm sure you both can come to some sort of agreement that doesn't involve shooting anyone."

The older man scowled. "Fine. But I don't want any of you in my backyard until this is resolved."

"It's not your backyard." The surveyor waved the piece of paper around, and I thought for a moment they were about to come to blows—or gunshots.

The portly guy, who I assumed was the developer, put up his hands. "It's fine. We can wait. Come on Stan. We'll come back another day to do this section. In the meantime, you can survey the rest of the property."

"But we need this line," Stan argued.

The developer shot him a warning glance, then reached out to grab his shoulder and turn him away from the homeowner. "We'll do it later. Come one. There's no sense in standing here and arguing about it until we find out which survey is in error and which one is correct."

Stan grumbled, stuffing the paper in his pocket and adjusting the weight of the tripod before following the developer. I watched them make their way through the overgrown weeds and brush, then turned to the homeowner.

"Are you okay?" I wanted to ask him what the heck he was thinking running out here to confront two men with a shotgun in hand. Who in the world thinks of that as their first response to a problem? Yes, he'd assumed they were trying to rob the place, but wouldn't a better idea have been to call the police?

"Yeah." He turned to face me, then smiled as he caught sight of Cagney. "Is this pretty girl yours? Who's a good girl? You're a good girl, that's who."

Cagney wiggled her whole body, coming in for some pats and scratching while I blinked at the quick transition from homestead defender to dog lover.

"No matter where the property line ends up being, you do realize that they are going to be out surveying in that field. And maybe digging," I said, thinking of the archeologist. "And maybe even putting up houses."

"Houses?" The man straightened from petting Cagney and scowled out into the field. "I don't want a bunch of houses out back behind my house."

"Nothing's been signed yet, but it's a possibility," I told him. "I don't know how many houses they're planning or where they'd put them, but it might happen. I'd think it might be nice to have some pretty yards and houses out here instead of all these weeds."

"I like the weeds," he countered. "I do a lot of bird watching off my back porch. They put up houses back here, all that would go away."

I nodded, thinking that there would still be birds, just perhaps different birds. "I'll talk to the owner cond look into the issue of the property line, but until it's resolved, I'd advise you not shoot anyone."

He grunted, hefting the shotgun. "It's full of rock salt. I'm not gonna kill anybody. At my age? No way I'm spending my last few years in a prison eating that horrible food. You wait here. I'm gonna go in and put this away and get you my name and phone number, so you can call me about all this."

I watched him head in, then looked around the backyard as Cagney sniffed one of the fence posts. This entire street of houses backed up to Suzette's field, and quite a few of them had fences that appeared in line with this man's. If there had been an error, then it might not just affect this man's property, it could affect every house on this block. Some people had gazebos and landscaping that might actually be on Suzette's property. In fact, there were two old apple trees right near the fence in this man's backyard that were probably a part of that orchard Suzette had said once stood here.

What a mess. I hoped it would be easily solved by a quick trip to the courthouse, but if this strip of land really was Suzette's, people might turn their anger toward her, and not whatever surveyor had made the error back in the sixties.

A shadowy figure materialized near one of the apple trees. It hovered for a while, then moved right through the fence into the field where it moved back and forth parallel to the backyards. I frowned, thinking that there were similarities between this ghost and the one that haunted Suzette's pond. They were both men, of about the same age, and they felt as if their spirits had been wandering here for about the same amount of time.

The man returned and handed me a slip of paper with his address, and contact information as well as when he'd purchased his house—well, give or take a few years. Evidently Mr. Floyd Ambrose wasn't quite sure if he'd bought it the year the Vietnam War ended or the year after, but I was pretty sure I could find what I needed at the courthouse using the property address.

"That man isn't the only one whose been sneaking around here," Mr. Ambrose informed me. "There's some woman as well. She's digging by the fence. Caught her trying to dig a hole by my apple tree and I told her to stay out of my yard."

"Did she leave?" I asked the man.

He scowled. "She argued with me for a while. Told me she had every right to dig there. Said the owner had given her permission or something. I didn't like it so I sat outside and watched her until she finally packed up and went somewhere else."

Ah. It must have been that Miranda woman from the Historical Society who'd offered to dig for artifacts that could help Suzette with the grant applications. But why would she be digging way out here, where the Hostenfelder property had once bordered the Millers'? This had been an apple orchard and a crop field. I couldn't imagine there being any useful artifacts on this part of the property.

I promised to call Mr. Ambrose as soon as I found anything out about the boundary line. As I made my way back to the house, I argued with myself over whether I should call Suzette or not. I hated to ruin her day with more property woes, but I felt a little odd doing land records searches without her knowledge or permission. Plus, I was pretty sure the developer would let her know there had been an issue with the property boundaries, if he hadn't already called her.

Finally I decided to text her. Later. Once she'd had a chance to get settled in at work for the day. Or maybe later tonight. This wasn't an emergency or anything. It wasn't like anyone was going to die over ten feet of land between two properties. It could wait.

CHAPTER 15

$\mathcal{O}$nce home, I got Cagney situated in her crate with food and water, then rushed to grab my bag and head out the door. I was going to be late for work. Again. As much as I enjoyed taking Cagney out this morning, our walk had extended a bit longer than I'd intended. Judge Beck was right about keeping the kids involved in Cagney's care. Last night he'd offered to do all the morning walks when the kids weren't with us, and had said he'd do evening walks if the kids had after school activities on their assigned days. Fitting the care for a dog into our lives would require some adjustment on everyone's part. If anything, the last two months had taught me that cats were a whole lot easier than dogs as far as pets went.

J.T. was actually in the office this morning. I burst through the door at five after, having broken a whole slew of speed limits trying to get in on time.

"Sorry," I grimaced over at him as I pulled my laptop out. "We've unexpectedly re-acquired a puppy and we're figuring out schedules to accommodate."

Molly squealed, spinning around in her chair to face me.

"Heather returned Cagney? You're keeping her? We'll have to bring Starsky over to play. He'll be so excited to see his sister again."

For Starsky, excitement meant a big yawn before a nap, but maybe Cagney could get her lazy brother moving a bit more.

"Well, you're going to be busy today, so I'm glad you didn't have to bring the puppy in with you," J.T. said as he plopped a file on my desk. "We are now officially doing service of process. And this is our first case."

I looked down at the file and knowing that "our first case" really meant "my first case."

"It's going to require the same type of research as the repossessions," J.T. said. "You'll need to dig a little for current address, job, and hours of work. We'll try to serve people at home first, so you may need to work late a few nights or get started early since most people aren't home between the hours of nine-to-five. If they're ducking service, you might need to catch them coming or going from home, or even at work."

I sighed, picking up the file. "People aren't going to shoot at me, are they? Or chase me down the street with a bat?"

J.T. rolled his eyes. "You're not repossessing their car, you're just handing them a paper, then making notes about the date, time, location, and exactly who was served."

"I'm still worried about them trying to shoot me," I insisted, leafing through the papers.

"I'll handle the first few," he told me. "You do the research, and I'll serve the paperwork. But with all of our other work, you might have to actually serve the paperwork yourself on some of these cases."

"Unless J.T. gets shot on the first few jobs," Molly chimed in.

"If J.T. gets shot, then I'm definitely not delivering these," I vowed.

J.T. blew out a breath. "If I get shot, then we'll all be out of business and unemployed. So let's hope that doesn't happen."

I held up my crossed fingers, only half joking about the getting-shot thing. There had been some close calls with the repossessions, but J.T. was right. We would just be handing over a piece of paper, and not trying to drive away with someone's car.

"I know it's more work," J.T. stated the obvious, "but it really compliments our services in skip tracing and repossession."

Molly and I did a lot of this kind of research already in finding debtors who'd defaulted on their payments. Credicorp and our other clients used that information to attempt to collect on the debt, but when their efforts weren't successful, they moved forward either with repossession, or a lawsuit for a judgement on the debt—possibly even wage garnishment. As much as I wanted to delve deeper into the private investigation side of our business, the reality was that this sort of work was what paid our salaries and kept the lights on. Bail Bonds fees were our next highest revenue source coming in at a distant second place, and actual investigative cases below that. Occasionally we had someone wanting to check on a potentially cheating spouse, or dig up information on a too-good-to-be-true new girlfriend or boyfriend. Not that I wanted murders and kidnappings and theft to be an everyday thing, but it was the investigative part of the job I really loved. Skip tracing was interesting, but finding people because they stopped paying their credit cards months ago, or had an unpaid hospital bill felt...icky. I wanted to track down the bad guys, and I had a hard time convincing myself that people with unpaid debts or defaulted car loans fell into the bad-guy territory.

"And tomorrow, we're filming," J.T. added.

My head jerked up at that. "Filming?"

A little over a year ago, J.T. had decided the best way to land his own reality series was to start a YouTube channel highlighting his promising investigative cases. "Gator" Pierson's videos were mostly filmed via cell phone and edited on his laptop with the acting done by employees and friends, although at times, J.T. had convinced local college film students to provide more professional production.

The videos were bad. Really bad. And they'd taken off, in part because we'd been involved in some high-profile cases—like finding out our mayor was a murderer, and discovering who'd killed Holt Dupree. The combination of some prominent investigations and the absolutely horrible acting and video quality had made "Gator" Pierson a bit of a cult internet celebrity. And J.T. was determined to capitalize on his fame.

"This video will be on the Prucilla Downing case," J.T. informed me.

I winced, not sure if I'd be playing myself in this reenactment, or the victim. After video comments had started mentioning me more often than "Gator," J.T. had begun taking artistic license with the cases, sometimes framing himself as the one discovering the killer. Quite a few of his videos weren't even cases we'd investigated, but ones I'd poked my nose into on my own, or cases solved completely by the local police. Thus "Gator's" video channel had slid more into fiction than actual reality. Which, I'd been told, wasn't all that unusual with reality television shows.

"I get to play Daisy," Molly chimed in.

"That would be because Daisy refuses to be in these videos," I added.

"*And* I'm playing the Golden Retriever breeder," she

continued. "And the neighbor. Hunter is going to be that angry adopter, and the Free the Fur guy."

I smiled, thinking that Molly's brother would probably enjoy the acting work, even if it was unpaid.

"Who's playing Gus Wilmont?" I asked, knowing J.T. wasn't about to be the villain of his own story."

"A kid from the community college. Dusty or Rusty or something." J.T. waved the question away. "I need you to play Prucilla Downing, Kay. It won't take a lot of time. Just the one scene of you arguing with the angry adopter guy, then another with you dead on the floor."

Great. That meant fake blood and probably wigs and costuming that J.T. had picked up at a yard sale somewhere—costuming that smelled like mothballs.

I'd started refusing to do J.T.'s videos, but he'd learned that if he paid me on the clock for my acting roles, and kept them to a minimum, I usually agreed. And honestly, playing a murdered woman in an amateur video would be better than running all over town trying to serve papers on some guy who'd ghosted on his credit card bills.

I sighed. "Fine. Just let me know when and where for tomorrow."

"I'll text you the details," he promised.

With that, J.T. headed out to meet with a client. Molly turned around to continue her skip trace work. I picked up the file to get started on the process serving stuff, but texted Suzette first, asking if the developer had let her know there'd been a scuffle this morning between the surveyor and a neighbor.

I'd barely hit send before my phone rang.

"Oh Kay," Suzette said. "Was it you that was there? The developer said there was some woman walking a dog who jumped into the middle of the argument."

"That was me. I'm so sorry this happened. I'm sure it's just a simple mistake somewhere down at the recording office," I told her.

She let out an audible breath. "I'm learning that 'simple' isn't a word that applies to this whole mess. The Developer is proceeding with the survey and he'll still give me an offer on those lots, but it'll be contingent on getting the property line verified. And that horrible woman with the Historical Society called him and told him she'd file a lawsuit if he tried to take out any building permits on that land."

"I really think you need to talk to a lawyer about the Historical Society," I told her. "I'll ask the judge to recommend someone for you."

She made a frustrated noise. "I'm ready to give up on the idea of selling those three acres. Maybe filing for the grants would be easier."

"Maybe. Maybe not," I cautioned her. "I still think you need to keep exploring all of your options, but that property line dispute is going to be a problem no matter which avenue you choose. I actually was going to research it for you, but I didn't want to go sticking my nose into it all without your permission."

"Oh, would you?" Her voice wavered a bit. "I'll pay you, Kay. You're right. That needs to be resolved and the records corrected. If not, it's going to be an issue for whoever inherits the property when I'm gone as well as in the grant process, or in any sale for future development."

I really hated charging Suzette for this sort of thing, but if I wanted to research the deeds, I'd need to do it during work hours at the courthouse. And I could hardly continue to put aside paying work to do favors for friends.

"I'll keep track of my time and expenses," I told her. "Is there a budget maximum? That way if I run into snags, I can call you first for authorization."

In reality, I just wanted to make sure I didn't bill over her maximum.

"Three hundred?" Suzette asked. "I don't know how much research would cost on a property where the deeds go back hundreds of years, so let me know if that's not enough."

"I'm sure that will be plenty," I assured her, making a mental note not to spend half that.

As much as I wanted to head on over to the courthouse there was other work that needed to be done first. I sorted out the repossession files I'd done last night for J.T. and organized them on his desk along with my notes for each case. After that, I did a search for a bail bond request and texted that to J.T. since those clients needed to know right away if we were going to post their bond or not. Then I picked up the file for process serving on Robert Vine. It was a five thousand dollar debt on a credit card he'd taken out four months ago, promptly run up to the max, and never paid a penny on. Looking through the paperwork, I realized most of the five grand had been in a cash advance, and the rest had been a balance transfer from another card.

With a sympathetic sigh, I pulled up his information on my laptop and saw that the poor guy was in a lot of trouble. Four bounced checks that he'd paid off right before they went to collections. Two other credit cards that he had closed and was making minimum payments on. Robert was drowning in debt, and I felt sorry for him. And guilty. I was about to make his life a whole lot more unhappy.

I dug around, this sort of investigative research feeling almost easy after a year of skip tracing. Robert Vine didn't live at the address the credit card company had been sending statements to. His social media accounts were locked down, and no amount of sneaky internet work on my part managed to get more than a few pictures of his dog and a few of cars at a racetrack.

By lunchtime, I was ready for a break. I sent a quick text to Violet, knowing that most of the administrative areas of the courthouse tended to either shut down at noon or have only one person left behind to eat a sandwich at their desk and handle any urgent requests. Molly offered to run out to the deli, so I gave her some money, my order, and kept digging through the internet for anything I could discover about Robert Vine.

By the time Molly had returned, I still didn't have a good address for the guy.

"Find anything?" Molly asked as she handed me my egg salad on whole wheat.

"Zip." I sighed. "I have where he works, assuming the credit reporting agencies have up-to-date information. It looks like it was last verified two months ago, so it's anyone's guess if he still is employed there or not."

"You're gonna call them?" she asked.

I knew she meant the company. "After lunch. I doubt they'll give me his home address without a court order, though."

I honestly did feel sorry for the man. He clearly was trying to turn things around, but taking out additional loans wasn't helping. Wasn't part of this the credit card company's fault? They'd given a man who was clearly struggling financially additional debt? Although in all fairness, Robert might have had a better credit score four months ago when he'd applied for the card.

My phone beeped, and I looked at the text. Violet was back from lunch and had already called down to the records division for the documents I needed as well as pulled old tax assessment records from her department.

I packed up my laptop and files. "I'm heading over to the courthouse. If J.T. comes in, tell him the repo info is on his desk, and that the details on the bail bonds review are there as well. He can call if he needs. I hope to be back here, but if I run late, I'll finish the process serving research tonight at home."

Molly waved at me. "Give Cagney a big smooch for me. And Taco. And Judge Beck."

I felt my face warm at the last comment, but just smiled. Outside of Daisy, I'd kept the details of my romance with the judge to myself. His kids knew, but I hadn't really wanted anyone else to. There was still a little part of me that worried it wouldn't last, and I didn't want to have to explain to all my friends and co-workers that we were no longer an "item."

I guess we'd been pretty obvious, though. His hand on my shoulder during our porch happy hour. The way we looked at each other. How we stood close together, our arms brushing as we spoke.

Everyone probably knew. And I'd just have to get used to that.

CHAPTER 16

Violet waved at me from behind the counter at the tax assessment office in the courthouse.

"I pulled all the tax data on Suzette's property, as well as the old Miller property. I didn't see anything indicating a change in boundary lines." She handed me a folder full of copies. "But we don't record the deed and survey data in our records. I can see the change in assessment when the land sales occurred during the development but nothing outside of that. So I went down to the land records division and pulled the old plats. There is definitely a discrepancy between the last survey done on the Hostenfelder property over a hundred years ago and the one done on the Miller property in 1960."

"Do you think there might have been a mistake in the 1960 survey?" I asked, flipping through the papers. "Or maybe there was some land sold to the Millers in the last hundred years that never got recorded?"

"It's a possibility. The houses that were built there were never part of Suzette's family's farm. They were on land that was part of the Miller farm. Suzette's land took a dog-leg around that section, then continue back a ways, so there's a chance the Hostenfelders might have sold that strip to the Millers at some point."

I frowned, not really understanding either the copies in the folder or the significance of what Violet was telling me.

"That's where the discrepancy occurred," she explained, seeing my confusion. "Currently the Miller plat and the Hostenfelder plat overlap. There was an error, but I can't tell which property deed the error occurred on."

"Is there any other place a survey might have been recorded?" I asked. "A hundred years is a long time. Maybe the agreement and the documents got lost somewhere, and that land really did transfer to the Millers."

Violet nodded. "It absolutely could have happened. I can order the archival documents from the state. Or we can ask the Locust Point Historical Society. They like to keep copies of all the original deeds and documents going back over three hundred years. But I warn you, there still might be discrepancies. It's ten feet, Kay. The Miller and the Hosten-felder families might have argued over that ten feet, but whatever agreement they came to probably was done on a handshake and never recorded. I'm finding out that was common back then."

I sighed, thinking this was a whole lot of work for ten feet. Suzette might just want to sign that strip of land away, but I wanted to do a little bit more research before I threw in the towel here.

With my bag full of the copies Violet had made for me, I headed to the Locust Point Historical Society next. I'd never been inside although I'd driven past the little building down on Main Street many times. Locust Point was a tiny town compared to neighboring Milford, but we did have a thriving downtown with a handful of antique shops, a deli, a pub, a bakery, and a salon in addition to the Historical Society office. I walked in and was a bit surprised to see the front part of the building housed a museum. Glass cases were filled with local artifacts displayed next to pictures and drawings. Informational plaques told the history of the town and explained the various items and photos. I was fascinated with one drawing that showed the town before it was even a town. The four founding families claimed the majority of the real estate on the map. The Hostenfelders had the largest of the properties, with the neighboring Millers a close second followed by the Schmidt farm and the Boville farm. There was a scattering of smaller farms that in the next map were gone, either absorbed into the larger farms, or part of a small cluster of buildings that was titled the Towne of Locust Point in a decorative, swirling script. I squinted at the boundary lines, but didn't know enough about cartography or surveying to tell the difference between these documents and the ones that Violet had given me from the courthouse records division.

Glancing at other maps didn't bring me any further enlightenment, but there was one theme that ran throughout the museum—the Hostenfelder family had been here throughout the history of Locust Point, and they were still here. The last exhibit showed a glossy photo of Suzette's house along with other pictures of her property. The plaque proudly noted that the house and the remaining acres of the original farm were still owned by the family.

I went back, looking at the displays specific to the Miller and Schmidt families. The Schmidts had started splitting their farm among family members just after the Revolutionary War and by the end of the nineteenth century, nothing remained of the original farm except for the old house and two acres. That was demolished in 1950, and ten single-story houses now stood where the Schmidt house had once been.

The Millers held on for longer. They had also sold a portion of their land roughly a hundred years ago, approximately the same time Suzette's ancestor sold off the section of their farm that became the houses on my street as well as my own beloved Victorian. According to the museum documents, the farms had sold off bits and pieces of land since that point. I felt for the two families, imagining their struggles to turn a profit farming and trying to support their families. By 1960 the Millers had thrown in the towel, selling the rest of their farm in its entirety for development. Suzette's family continued to sell off an acre here and there, but had managed to hold on to the house and the remaining bit for the last forty years.

Once more I wondered if Floyd Ambrose wasn't the only homeowner whose boundary lines were at odds with what the Hostenfelder deed showed. I hated to blame whoever had done the Miller surveys back in 1960. There was a good chance that the one for Suzette's property was in error, or that the property lines had been modified and the sales documents had never formally been recorded. I was a suspicious woman, and my imagination immediately shifted to fraud, where the Millers paid a surveyor to move their property lines just a bit in order to make a little extra money on their land sale.

But wouldn't Suzette's family have noticed? From what I could tell by the pictures and drawings, the Hostenfelder livestock and fences had been on the opposite side of their farm, and the area bordering the Miller farm had been that huge apple orchard. By 1960, Suzette's grandparents were only part time farmers, having taken jobs in town to provide a more reliable income along with the benefits those jobs provided. Her grandfather had been a welder, and her grandmother had taught school until she'd retired. By the end of the twentieth century, the last of even their small livestock was gone, and the orchard had been long gone. Mr. Ambrose's property backed up to a field of weeds when his and the other houses had been built.

"Can I help you with anything?" a familiar voice asked.

I turned around to see Ann Baker behind me, a pleasant, if somewhat stiff, smile on her face. Was it Ann Baker? Or Miranda Cook? For a second I was confused, trying to remember which was which since I hadn't actually been introduced to the two when they'd been at Suzette's and only knew their names from the business cards they'd left behind.

Ann. I remembered Suzette said the older one's name was Ann.

"I'm Kay Carrera with Pierson Investigative and Recovery Services." I hesitated a second to see if the woman remembered me, but no sign of recognition flickered in her eyes. "I'm doing some research on the behalf of a client about a boundary line dispute, and I was hoping you could help me."

One of Ann's eyebrows rose. "You're probably better off going to the courthouse records division. We have some survey data from before the Civil War, but nothing on houses built in the last century."

"Their records conflict," I told her. "And it looks like the discrepancy might go back to when the properties were originally held by the Hostenfelder and the Miller families."

Now she looked intrigued. "Still, there would be records of those surveys at the courthouse. We only have copies of the same documents for our history exhibit."

"I already have the official surveys," I told her. "But I think there might have been a sort of informal or even handshake agreement on the property lines between the Hostenfelder farm and the Miller farm. I'm hoping it might have been written down in a journal or a letter somewhere."

Suzette had journals and letters from her side of the family, but she'd read most of those and would have noticed a land transfer if it had been mentioned. The Millers were long gone. Their family hadn't lived here in decades, and I wasn't sure I could track down their descendants, or who might have their old family documents—if they'd even bothered to keep them. But I could absolutely see Ann or her predecessor snatching them up in the 1960's or even at an estate or yard sale. As one of the main founding families of the town, whoever was running the Locust Point Historical Society would really have wanted those documents to preserve and hold.

"We do have quite a lot of letters and such from the Miller family as well as some that were donated from the Hostenfelder family," Ann told me. "Not all of them are digitized, though. We've been working through them, scanning and making notes, but it's slow going. If you had a better idea of a date—even a year—that you suspect the transaction was made, we might be able to find it. Otherwise we'd be looking for that proverbial needle in a haystack, and we might not be able to locate the appropriate reference document without years of searching."

I frowned, thinking that Suzette and Mr. Ambrose might just need to come to a compromise on this. I was sure neither of them wanted a lengthy legal battle that, from where I stood, would be nearly impossible to resolve in anyone's favor without additional data.

Wait.

"You have letters and documents from the Hostenfelder family?" I'd thought Suzette had kept all of those. She'd referenced her family journals and letters back when I'd been looking into the Stevens murder from 1926.

"Oh yes." Ann's smile was smug. "We have letters that they wrote to others in the town, as well as some of the contracts they signed, plus items that have been donated to us over the years. The Hostenfelder family has always taken the preservation of town history seriously, and while they've retained most of their family diaries, they've graciously shared some documents as well as family items with us. Some of our earliest drawings of the town and photographs came from the Hostenfelders."

I guess that shouldn't have been a surprise. Suzette's grandmother had died only a few years ago. Until that point there were plenty of others who might have chosen to donate some of their extensive family records to benefit the museum of the town's history.

"I'll need to discuss all this with my client," I murmured, thinking that it was increasingly improbably anyone would be able to know exactly what had happened between the Hostenfelders and the Millers in regards to their property line. The older deeds showed that ten feet in the Hostenfelder farm. Without any paperwork showing a transfer, a judge would probably rule in Suzette's favor, assuming that the Miller property line was an error that wasn't caught at the time of the development. But knowing Suzette, I was willing to bet the woman wouldn't push the issue of the extra ten feet. She'd probably sign away that extra land to Mr. Ambrose and the other residents, but it was her decision to make.

"Well, just in case you want a little late-night reading, we have some transcripts of the Miller documents for sale." Ann waved a hand over a display of thin, printed books as if she were Vanna White. "I can also print out what Miranda has been scanning. Not all of it has been transcribed yet, so you'll need to deal with smudged cursive writing from old letters, but it might be helpful."

"It would be helpful," I mused. I had a ton of work to do, and knew that reading old letters and documents from the last two hundred years wasn't something I really should be squeezing into my agenda. But something made me say yes.

Maybe buried in the letters was a note from a Miller long dead that explained the inconsistency in the surveys.

Ann pulled three books off the shelf and handed them to me, then asked me to wait as she went into a back room. I heard the whirr of a printer and spent the next ten minutes looking at broken pottery, rusted bayonet tips, and faded letters. By the time Ann came out with the printouts, I'd moved on to a display of aerial photos showing how various properties had changed over the years.

"Fifty-two thirty seven," she cheerfully announced as she rang up my purchases.

I stifled a gasp, then handed over my credit card doing some quick math in my head. The little booklets were twelve dollars each, and I'd assumed the print-outs would only be a few dollars. I guess not.

Wincing a little at the cost, I signed for the bundle of books and papers, put them in my bag, and headed back to work where I continued to our research process serving cases, which had grown to three while I'd been gone.

CHAPTER 17

At a little after five o'clock, I packed up for the day, hurrying home and flinging everything aside to let a barking Cagney out of her cage. I didn't even bother to take my coat off before snapping the pup's leash on and dashing out for her evening walk. Taco darted through the door as well, running off in the opposite direction. I worried about him when he was out of the house, but I knew he'd be on the front porch when Cagney and I returned home from our walk, yowling for his dinner.

I was half-jogging down the street, towed behind an energetic Cagney, when I saw Suzette's car in her drive. Deciding I might as well cross one thing off my evening's to-do list, I headed up her front steps, smiling as I heard Gus barking from inside.

Suzette opened the door and the French Bulldog darted out between her legs, snorting and snuffling as he danced around Cagney. My pup was equally excited to see him, tangling her leash as she hopped and spun in play.

"Do you have a second?" I asked Suzette. "I've got some

paperwork from the courthouse to bring by later, but I thought I'd go ahead and fill you in on what I found out."

"Of course. Come in." She stood aside and I lurched through the doorway as Gus ran inside the house and Cagney ran after him, only the leash stopping the her from running through the kitchen.

"Did you want some coffee? Iced tea? Wine?" Suzette asked.

"No, thank you. I'm good." I stooped to unsnap Cagney's leash, warning her to be on her best behavior. The dog ignored me, racing off after Gus.

Suzette and I sat at the kitchen table and in between the noise of barking dogs and squeaking toys, I told her about my research and what I was guessing had happened to confuse the placement of the property line.

Suzette sighed. "My family was very close with the Millers. They were good friends for many generations before the Millers sold the remaining bit of their farm a few years before my dad was born. I'm willing to bet my ancestors gave or traded those extra feet to the Millers for some reason or another, and no one ever bothered to register the change at the courthouse. Let me know what I need to do and I'll just sign those ten feet over to Mr. Ambrose."

"Let's wait a bit on that," I cautioned her. "His property might not be the only one affected, and I don't want you to set a precedent and end up giving away land without doing research first. I picked up some stuff at the Historical Society I want to go over before you make any decisions. They have a whole lot of letters and documents from the Millers, and there might be something in there about the land."

Suzette sighed. "So whatever agreement happened between their family and mine might only affect Mr. Ambrose's land, or it could affect all the houses on that block."

"And it might have just been a temporary arrangement," I cautioned her. "I don't want you giving land away if the deal between your family and the Millers was only supposed to be for ten or twenty or thirty years, and somehow that was forgotten when they sold."

"If that's the case, I might be tempted to just let the land go." Suzette sighed. "I don't want to have bad feelings between neighbors and me. I plan on living here the rest of my life and don't want people holding a grudge because they think I took property away from them—even if it's just ten feet."

"Ten feet *is* a lot when your plot is less than a quarter acre," I comment. "You might want to bring in a title company and have the land surveyed on your own, then when all the data is in, you can make your decision."

She frowned. "I'm going to be honest with you, Kay, since you're my friend. A survey and research from a title company might be more than I can afford. And it would delay the sale of any acreage to the developer if I decide to go that route."

"The developer might not want to make an offer if they're worried they might face lawsuits over where the boundaries are on their purchase," I warned. "And they may back out entirely until this is resolved—meaning they'd want *you* to resolve it."

"Ugh, this is so frustrating!" Suzette ran an agitated hand through her hair. "Okay. I'll call the developer in the morning and let him know that this might be a problem, just to see what he says. If he backs out or wants to delay, then I'll pursue the grants and deal with the boundary dispute later. Actually, I might just go ahead and fill out the paperwork for the grants tonight. It's looking more and more like that's the better option here."

"And that brings me to something else." I told her about

what I'd discussed with Matt on Sunday, and how we wanted to run a fundraiser at her house and property. "The judge's kids are on board to help, and so am I, as well as Matt and Judge Beck. It could be a great way to raise money for the fence at the very least, and maybe even some of the pond restoration."

She stared down at the table for a few seconds, and when she looked up, I saw tears sparkling in her eyes. "Thank you, Kay. Even if we just raise enough for a fence, I'll sleep better at night. I'll gratefully accept everyone's help in running a fundraising event."

I grinned, happy that I'd been able to at least give Suzette something positive along with the bad news regarding the boundary line.

Suzette stood. "I was about to take Gus for a walk out back when you arrived. Olive is working late tonight, so I swung by her place and picked Gus up, not wanting him to be cooped up in a crater longer than necessary."

I got up as well. "Then I'll get out of your hair. Thanks for letting me drop in like this."

"Oh anytime." She waved my words away. "Why don't you come with me out back for a walk? Cagney and Gus will both get more exercise chasing each other around than if they're on their own."

That was true, and Cagney sure could use the extra workout. In spite of our extended walk this morning, she was bursting with energy. I now understood why Heather had struggled to keep the dog exercised, especially when the kids were gone.

"Cagney and I would love to walk with you and Gus," I told Suzette.

She dug in a drawer for her dog's harness and I walked over to the kitchen island where an assortment of items were arrayed.

"What's this?" I fingered the rusted hinges, the bent nails, and the few other metal items that I couldn't even begin to identify."

"Stuff that lady from the Historical Society dug up from my land." Suzette told me. "She's been here every day since Sunday, digging around the old barn and in the field. She even brought metal detectors and some sort of electronic equipment. She keeps looking at notes in a little book and on her phone, then searching and digging. Usually she's waiting for me when I get home with an assortment of stuff that she's found, but she must have left early today."

"It's kind of cool," I told her, lying a little bit. It *was* interesting that there were little scraps of everyday life scattered around the property—things that once belonged to those who'd come before us. But old hinges and bent, rusted nails weren't really all that exciting.

Suzette grabbed a leash off the wall and called for Gus before turning back to me. "Really, it's just junk. I should be grateful. She's been here all day every day, and I can't imagine how she keeps it up when this is all she's finding. If she finds anything important, it might influence my ability to get a grant. But it feels weird, like she's literally digging into my family's personal life. Plus, so far all she's found is rubbish—not particularly valuable rubbish either."

I shot her a sympathetic glance, knowing how private Suzette was. She'd let me into her life as a friend, as well as others in the neighborhood, but she was a person that limited who she trusted with her heart. Family meant so much to her. It was one of the reasons her grandmother had willed her the house and property instead of letting it go to one of the other relatives. Having a property developer and surveyors roaming across her property must bother her. And having someone from the Historical Society scanning her property and digging up items obviously bothered her as well.

"Are you going to be okay with this event I'm proposing?" I asked her, suddenly worried that so many strangers tromping through her house and property would be too much for Suzette.

She took a deep breath and let it out. "Yes. It'll be fine. Honestly, I *want* the community to love this place as much as I do. It's more than mine, it belongs to the town in a way. My ancestors and this farm are an important part of the history of Locust Point, and my preserving it isn't just for selfish reasons.

I thought back on what Ann had said earlier. "When I swung by the Historical Society, Ann mentioned that she had letters and journals from your family as well as the Millers."

Suzette nodded. "Grandmother gave a bunch of stuff to them for research and for the museum, and I did the same when I moved in and started going through things. There's so much here. I wanted to keep the stuff from my grandmother and her mother, as well as a few other things, but I worried what might happen if there was a fire or a flood. Or if I suddenly died. They'll scan and archive everything, and that's important to me. It's also important that some things be available to the public as part of the town's history."

I nodded, understanding exactly what she was saying.

"Do *you* want to share some of your family's story during the tours?" I asked, thinking the attendees might be just as interested in her tales as those of the local Historical Society.

"I do." She smiled. "I've been going through some of Grandma's and my great grandmother's journals and notes, trying to put together a little picture of what life was like seventy years ago as well as a hundred years ago. The other ladies can talk about the architectural styling, and early settlers to the area, and all that, but I want to share what it was like to struggle to support a family farming in the nine-teenth and early part of the 20th century, as well as what it was like to make the hard decision to sell off over half of the original acreage to development."

"I think that will really help bring in guests," I assured her. "People want to know the personal details. They'll want to know what quilts your great great grandmother made, the canned goods your grandmother was famous for, about the apple orchard and the Christmas geese they raised and sold. That's the history that Locust Point was built on, and that's what will interest people."

I bent down to snap Cagney's leash on and waited while Suzette struggled to get a squirming Gus into his harness and hook on his leash. We walked out the back door, and as soon as we were a decent distance from the back door, we turned both dogs loose and watched them run big circles around us as we walked the overgrown acres. Suzette had a clicker that she used to supplement her call when Gus strayed too far. Smart little guy that he was, he came racing right back, his little legs pumping with surprising speed. Cagney wasn't as well trained, but she followed her buddy when he returned. I made a mental note to ask Suzette and Olive who they'd used for Gus's obedience training classes and maybe pick up a clicker myself.

When we were heading back, the two dogs ran toward the pond, weaving in and out of the long marshy grasses and briars that grew up from the thick mud surrounding the banks. Suzette called and clicked, and Gus came running back, but this time Cagney didn't.

I could see her rustling through the brush, in spite of the fact that her brown fur blended perfectly with the pre-spring foliage. With an apologetic glance at Suzette, I jogged over to the pond, calling my dog. Cagney ignored me.

I blew out a frustrated breath and carefully picked my

way through the stickers and tall grass, nearly falling on the slick half-inch of melted mud on top of the frozen ground. Frozen was good. If we hadn't been experiencing such a late freeze, then this whole area would be deep sucking mud, and I would have lost a sneaker, if not my entire leg trying to get in here. Heck, I'd probably have found Cagney up to her nose in quick-mud.

A shadowy form materialized to my left, nearly giving me a heart attack. The figure hovered nearby. I assumed at first that it was the ghost of the Civil War soldier, but then I realized this was a different ghost. A man, but an older man than the Civil War soldier had been at the time of his death. Plus this was someone who had died more recently than a hundred and fifty years ago.

I tried to ignore the ghost, thinking that Suzette must have all sorts of spirits haunting this place, and kept searching for my dog.

"Cagney!" I grumbled a few words under my breath as I pushed my way through the weeds, falling face-first as I stumbled into a hole.

Stupid groundhogs, I thought, even though I couldn't imagine this being a good spot for a groundhog hole. Either way, I was filthy, my hands, knees, and the front of my jacket covered with mud in addition to my shoes. The only good thing about my current situation was that Cagney must have heard me fall and had come back, something about the size of a hubcap in her mouth. Dropping it, she ran over to me and licked my face, pushing her warm furry body against mine for leverage as I struggled to my feet. I quickly snapped the leash onto her collar as soon as I stood.

"What did you find, girl?" I took a few tentative steps over to where she'd dropped the hubcap-thing. Only it wasn't a hubcap. Holding tight to Cagney's leash, I bent over and picked up a drone. The thing was covered in tangled grasses, a piece of ice stuck to one side. I guess I didn't need to buy a pair of hip waders after all. I looked the thing over, wondering if it was still functioning or nothing more than a piece of junk. Either way, it would be interesting to see if I could trace it back to the owner through the serial number or something, if nothing more than so Suzette could know who was nosing around her property pre-dawn last Friday.

Tucking the thing under my elbow, I adjusted Cagney's leash, then looked around to determine the best way out of this mess of mud and briars. That's when I saw a trampled patch of grass at the edge of the still ice-covered pond.

It took me a second to process what exactly I was seeing. There, among the crushed grasses and broken briars lay a body—a wire-thin man with dark hair, wearing loose fitting jeans and a puffy parka. He was facedown in the pond, the ice broken around his head with his dark hair floating in the marshy water. Both arms were outstretched and his legs together, giving him an eerie Jesus-on-the-cross stance. Blood decorated the water, the ice, his hair, and the foliage surrounding him.

And next to the man, lying parallel to his body, was a surveyor's tripod.

CHAPTER 18

I sent Suzette inside with the dogs and the drone while I remained with the body. Knowing better than to touch anything, I tried to remain as still as possible. Trampled grass and briars might be a clue, and I didn't want to disturb any more of the foliage around the pond than Cagney and I already had. The sun was rapidly setting and soon I wouldn't be able to see more than a few feet ahead of me, especially since the moon wouldn't rise until late morning. I didn't want to ruin any evidence, so I held very still and waited. And that gave me a lot of time to stare at the body and think.

Stan. The developer guy had called the surveyor Stan, and even facedown in the pond I was pretty sure of his identity. The tripod was a giveaway, as was his thin build, the dark hair that was past due for a cut, and the baggy clothing. Who else would be on Suzette's property carrying survey equipment and wearing the same clothes I'd seen him in this morning? The only people with a reason to be here besides Suzette and Olive were the developer, the surveyor, and Miranda from the Historical Society—the woman who'd been digging up broken hinges and rusted nails.

"What happened, Stan?" I whispered.

The ghost who'd been nearby even before I'd stumbled across the body moved closer, staring down at his corpse with a mixture of sadness and annoyance. Of all the dangerous professions in the world that were liable to get a person killed, surveying was pretty far down the list.

Had this been an accident? The mud was a slick half inch on top of ice, and there were patches of marshy water where a person could easily break through and fall. Had he slipped or tripped, and banged his head on something, knocking him out so that he drowned? If so, then why was the injury on the back of his head, but he was facedown in the water? Had he hit his head, then rolled over in an attempt to get to his feet before passing out? I hoped so, because the only other theory I had was murder.

But who would have murdered him? Floyd Ambrose had definitely threatened the man this morning, but that had been with a shotgun full of rock salt. This was a blow to the head, and although I didn't want to discount Mr. Ambrose's ability or motive, he didn't seem in the physical shape to chase a thin, young man halfway across Suzette's property, then whack him in the back of the head with enough force to kill him. No, I could see Mr. Ambrose firing his shotgun toward the sky, maybe shuffling to his fence, then stopping to wave his fist in the air, declaring the trespasser should "keep off his lawn", but not murder.

And why was the surveyor *here*, in this particular place? Suzette was considering the sale of the outer parts of her property. The pond was fairly close to the back of the house and Suzette had been undecided on whether she'd wanted to include those acres in any sale. Had the developer talked to Suzette about potentially buying more land? Or asked the surveyor to mark it out, just in case he wanted to offer for this section as well? That might explain why the surveyor had been here, but not who would have been lurking just outside of Suzette's backyard with motive to kill the man.

I frowned. Trespassers did occasionally cut across these fields. But I couldn't see Stan confronting a trespasser, or one being upset enough about being called out to kill the man. Maybe he *had* just fallen, then passed out when trying to get up, only to drown. Maybe this was an accident. A terrible accident.

But right on the heels of Travis nearly drowning in the same pond? It seemed an odd coincidence.

The sirens sounded in the distance, growing louder then abruptly silenced once they entered the residential area of our neighborhood.

After a few minutes of silence in the company of a body and his ghost, I stood on my tip-toes, hoping to be able to see if someone was coming through the tall grasses. I caught a glimpse of two men walking across the back lawn. One I recognized as Miles even at this distance. The other man I didn't know. Right behind them was Suzette.

"I put the dogs in the spare bedroom so I could come out when the police got here," she called out as the three of them approached. "I also called Bernard Long, the developer, and the Historical Society office.

I frowned. "The Historical Society office?"

"I don't know if Miranda came out today to dig or not, but I wanted to check. If she was here, maybe she saw something."

It was a good idea. Suzette was the one thinking about possible witnesses here while I was mulling over whether Stan's ghost could somehow communicate whether he'd died by accident, or by someone's hand.

"Hey, Kay," Miles called out. "Are you cold? Is it okay for

you to stay where you are? Detective Toots and I want to take some pictures before you get out of the grasses."

I smiled, thinking of how sweet Miles was to worry that my feet were submerged in icy water, or that I might be chilled from standing here so long. "I'm okay. When I came in here I didn't see any trampled grasses. I'm pretty sure he came in from a different direction than I did, but I didn't want to mess anything up by moving around."

Wait. Detective *Toots*? We were a tiny town. Our policing was through the Sheriff's department, with assistance from larger, neighboring Milford.

"Where's Detective Keeler?" I asked. Desmond Keeler was a detective out of Milford and the bane of my existence. But he *was* an amazing detective, and I trusted both his judgement and his investigative skills. I had no idea who this Toots man was.

And what an unfortunate name. Toots. Did his family have a chronic flatulence problem? Or perhaps they were trumpet players?

"We've had enough murders in Locust Point over the year to get the funding for our own detective," Miles told me.

He didn't sound happy about that. I knew Miles respected Keeler. Either he didn't like the idea of bringing someone new in right now, or he didn't have the same level of respect toward this man. Although, Miles did tend to dislike change. It could be that he was grumpy over having a new detective, and he just needed to give the man a chance.

Both men came through the grass, little digital cameras clicking as they made their way toward me. They paused beside me, taking pictures of the area as well as the body.

"Pickford, nobody touches anything until the techs get here," Toots commanded. "I'm going to take this woman back to the house and interview her as well as the other woman. You stand guard here."

I blinked, then shot a wide-eyed glance at Miles.

He grimaced. "*This woman* is Kay Carrera. She's a private investigator who has been integral in the solving of several high-profile murders in the area. Judge Nathanial Beck currently resides at her home."

"I don't care if she's living with the Pope," Toots snapped. "This woman needs to come with me back to the house."

My eyebrows shot up. Okay, then. My expectations for Detective Toots had just plummeted about a thousand feet below sea level.

I might have my doubts about the guy, but he was a detective and he had been assigned to this case, so I shot Miles a sympathetic glance, then followed Toots as he stomped his way out of the marsh.

Suzette was waiting for us on the other side of the briars and grass. She was twisting her hands together in front of her, her face pale. I tried to smile reassuringly at her, but I didn't have it in me. At least Travis had been alive when she'd found him. Two tragic accidents on her property within one week, one of them resulting in a death. Poor Suzette. I wouldn't be surprised if she threw in the towel after all of this, selling completely out to the developers like the Millers had done.

I motioned for Suzette to come along and the pair of us followed Detective Toots into her house. The man made himself right at home, sprawling in one of her chairs at the kitchen table and pointing for us to take a seat.

I glared at the disrespect, but kept my mouth shut, sitting next to Suzette and opposite the man.

He got out a notepad and a pen, scribbled down a few things, then turned to Suzette.

"Tell me your full name and your whereabouts today," he commanded.

My friend's eyebrows rose and she shot me a puzzled

glance. I was equally confused. Surely Toots didn't consider her a suspect?

Suzette complied, telling the detective how she'd stayed at Olive's last night, then gone to work early. She said that she'd left work around three thirty, gone to pick up Gus at Olive's house, and been home by a little after four.

"Do you always leave work so early?" Toots asked. "And why did you decide to leave early today in particular?"

Suzette flushed. "No, I don't always leave so early, but I've had a lot going on this last week and have been using flex time to deal with it. I wanted to get home early today to go over applications I'm considering filling out for a grant."

"Did that man surprise you? Maybe you were out walking and were startled by a trespasser? So you hit him in the head? You're a young woman living alone. I can imagine that seeing a man lurking around your property would be a frightening thing."

Where the heck was Toots going with this?

"First off," I interjected, "Suzette and I were both walking our dogs together. She wasn't carrying a bat or any other item that she could have used to hit the man. Secondly, *I* was the one that found the body, not Suzette. And third, this isn't some random trespasser. He's a surveyor. He's a surveyor hired by Smyth and Long Homes because my friend here is contemplating selling off some of her acreage. Even if she'd come across the man while he was still upright and breathing, she wouldn't have been frightened because there have been people on and off her property the last few days. She would have expected to see him here. And the guy had a surveying tripod. What scary trespasser carries around a surveying tripod?"

"Did you hit him over the head with his tripod?" Toots asked Suzette.

For Pete's sake. "She didn't even see him. At all," I insisted.

Suzette held up her hands. "I wasn't here until four o'clock this afternoon. Kay texted me at work and when I called her back, she told me that she'd seen the developer and the surveyor this morning having an argument with one of the neighbors over the property line. And yes, I expected there to be a surveyor on my property either today or tomorrow. I wouldn't have been surprised to see him, or Mr. Long, or one of the ladies from the Historical Society, or people from any of the three companies I'd called requesting a quote on fencing and on work on the pond."

"Ah yes, the neighbor." Toots consulted his notes, then leaned in, fixing Suzette with a hard stare. "We received a complaint this morning that a man identified as Floyd Ambrose had threatened Stan Milbourn and Bernard Long with a shotgun."

"A shotgun he said was loaded with rock salt," I countered. Although Floyd Ambrose might have been lying about the rock salt, I doubted he was. "Regardless, the victim doesn't have any torn clothing or wounds I could see that are consistent with being shot with a shotgun blast—rock salt or not. He was hit in the back of the head."

"The other wounds might be on the front of him," Toots snapped at me.

I held back an eye roll with heroic effort. "So you're saying Mr. Ambrose had a second confrontation with the surveyor, and shot him head-on. Then the surveyor managed to run all the way back to the pond without pausing to call the police, only to end up facedown at the edge of the pond with a wound in the back of his head?"

The detective scribbled something on his notepad. I squinted, trying to read the words, and could make out something about looking for a blood trail through the field from Floyd Ambrose's yard. It was definitely something he should check for, but Toots was an idiot and I had no faith in his ability to find the killer. Where the heck had this detective been hired from? Someone at the sheriff's office clearly hadn't done a good job of checking references.

"It could have been an accident," Suzette chimed in.

"Or you could have murdered him," Toots responded.

This time I did roll my eyes. "Suzette would have no reason to murder a surveyor for the developer she's considering selling her land to."

"Maybe he was blackmailing her on where he could place the property lines," Toots suggested.

"That's ridiculous. She could just refuse to be blackmailed, then hire her own surveyor instead. Suzette didn't murder the guy. She didn't even know he was there."

"Maybe she did," he countered.

I blew out a breath. "Then why would she invite me to go for a walk with her and the dogs? Really detective. She was gone all day. She has an alibi with witnesses up until 3:30 this afternoon."

He scribbled a few more notes, then turned to me. Although I didn't particularly want this guy's attention, at least he wasn't hounding Suzette any more.

"Tell me about the argument between Mr. Ambrose, the developer, and the surveyor," he commanded.

I went over everything that had happened this morning, including my call with Suzette, and my research today.

"Yes, Mr. Ambrose was angry. He's an old man, and he looked out his window early in the morning to see two men over his fence and in his yard. He also said he'd had a confrontation previously with the woman from the Historical Society who was digging near his fence—a confrontation that didn't involve a shotgun. That was probably on Sunday. But I don't think Floyd Ambrose would have actually shot anyone, let alone hit them in the back of the head. I told him I was going to contact Suzette and that I was sure the matter of the disputed boundary line could be solved through some quick research at the courthouse. It hasn't even been twenty-four hours. I'm certain he would have waited to see what the documentation revealed before going after the surveyor."

Toots frowned. "Even if the surveyor showed back up this afternoon, setting up equipment in his yard again? Maybe he saw the man, and just lost his temper."

I thought about my brief interaction with Floyd Ambrose and couldn't really refute that theory. Bernard Long *had* told the surveyor to stay away from that particular part of the property line for today, but Stan might have gone back. And Mr. Ambrose might have been upset enough to grab his shotgun and confront him once more. But then why was Stan found over by the pond, and why did he have a wound in the back of his head?

"Where were you at…" Toots looked at his notes, "…three o'clock this afternoon to four o'clock?"

"Me?" Oh, good grief, was I a suspect now? "I was at work from two until five o'clock, and got home a little after that. I think it was about five twenty when I got here to see Suzette."

Miles popped his head in the back door. "The techs are here, Detective Toots. Did you want to speak to them before they get started? And we're having to set up lights around the crime scene."

Toots stood, then waved a hand at Suzette and me. "I'll continue questioning you two later."

"Don't leave town?" I asked after he'd left.

Suzette snorted. "That would be difficult to comply with since my job is technically outside of Locust Point. Yours too. And heaven forbid we decide to get sushi or something."

"I don't have high hopes for this guy solving the crime," I told her.

"Then you'll just have to do it for him." Suzette stood.

"And do it quick before the fool arrests me and throws me in jail."

"Or me," I said. "Or Mr. Ambrose."

"I'm not one hundred percent sure on Mr. Ambrose's innocence," Suzette said. "I'd like to think it might have been an accident, but the prisons are full of people who got angry and killed someone."

"Eighty-year-old men?" I asked her. "Maybe this had nothing to do with your property or the neighbors. Maybe Stan was sleeping with a married woman and her husband found out. Maybe he owed someone a whole lot of money, or was just in the wrong place at the wrong time."

Suzette sighed. "You're right. But either way, I think you better solve this murder before Toots throws all of us in jail."

CHAPTER 19

*B*ernard Long followed Suzette into the kitchen, sitting down in the chair the detective had vacated ten minutes ago. His face was pale, his hands shaking.

"It's Stan? Are you sure it's Stan? After I got your message, some detective called me and told me to come down here. Said my surveyor was found dead in the pond. I tried to reach Stan right after I got the call and he didn't pick up, but I just can't believe…what happened?" he asked.

Toots had called the developer and asked him to come *here*? I frowned, wondering why he hadn't had Mr. Long go down to the station, or why he hadn't sent an officer over to pick the man up. Even if Toots wanted a positive ID, it didn't seem proper for it to be here with crime scene techs and the medical examiner all hovering around Suzette's pond.

"I'm not *absolutely* positive it was Stan," I told the developer. "I found a man facedown in the water at the edge of the pond with a wound on the back of his head. He was wearing the same clothes the surveyor had on this morning, was the same build, and had a surveyor's tripod next to him, so I'm pretty sure it was Stan even though I didn't see the man's face."

The developer's gaze focused on me. "You're the woman from this morning. You're the one who came over when Stan and I were arguing with that homeowner—the one with the gun." He sucked in a breath. "You don't think *he's* the one who did this, do you? I told Stan to stay away from that property line today and just do that section later, but he can be such a stubborn guy when it comes to things."

"It might have been an accident," I told him, even though I wasn't convinced that was the case. "When was the last time you talked to Stan? Was he really here all day?"

Bernard Long nodded. "I wanted him to take down a lot of measurements and data so I could run different mock-ups. How many houses we could put in, where they should go, where the drives and access roads should be—that sort of thing." He pulled his phone out of his pocket and scrolled through it. "He called me around three o'clock. I remember being annoyed that he was still here and not done yet. He told me it had taken longer because a lot of people were coming out to see what he was doing. He said some woman was pestering him. He complained that she was watching him and asking a lot of questions, disrupting his work or something. I told him to wrap it up and get out before four, because I didn't want Ms. Hostenfelder to come home from work and have him still setting stuff up on her property."

I frowned. "Did he say which neighbors came out to talk to him? Anything that might pinpoint the woman who'd been pestering him?"

Clearly Mr. Ambrose wasn't the only person home in the middle of the day who'd seen the surveyor at work. If it *was* murder, and the killer wasn't a jealous ex-husband or a loan shark, then maybe the elderly homeowner wouldn't be the only other suspect.

The developer shook his head. "Not that I remember. Of course, I wasn't paying much attention. Stan's a good guy, but he complains all the time about everyone. I tune him out unless it's urgent. I was glad I was here this morning when that guy came out with a shotgun though." His expression sobered. "Wish I'd been here this afternoon as well. Maybe Stan would still be alive."

He clearly thought Stan's confrontational manner was what led to his death. I thought so as well, although I was trying to keep an open mind. It *could* have been an accident.

Suzette's doorbell rang again, and with an apologetic glance, she went to answer it. This time she returned with the younger woman from the Historical Society following behind her. Miranda was just as pale and shaken as Bernard Long. She took the seat beside me, and Suzette lowering herself into the fourth chair. I had a moment's thought about how there were no remaining seats for Detective Toots or any other law enforcement who might come in wanting to question us, but seating was really the last thing I should be thinking of right now.

"I got a call from some detective telling me I was supposed to meet him here," Miranda said. "Something about a body?"

I nodded, annoyed that Toots was turning my friend's kitchen into a makeshift police interview room.

"We're pretty sure it's the surveyor," Suzette told her. "Were you here digging today? Did you hear or see anything?"

She shook her head, then frowned. "No…I mean, I did see a guy surveying, but he wasn't anywhere near where I was working so I didn't pay any attention to him. It was cold and I wasn't having much luck, so I packed up around noon and went back to the office. As I was leaving, I heard a noise like an explosion gunshot or something. There aren't any shooting ranges around here and I couldn't imagine anyone hunting inside the city limits, so I figured it was a car or construction and left."

"You heard a gunshot and didn't tell anyone?" I exclaimed. This didn't look good for Floyd Ambrose. Although Stan hadn't looked like he'd been shot. Maybe Floyd had shot into the air to scare him away? And then Stan had tripped and fallen while he was running, and hit his head? Although why would he be running through the tangle of vegetation around the pond.

"I didn't think it was a gunshot." Miranda scowled at me. "But now that someone's been murdered, I'm wondering if it was a gunshot after all."

My phone beeped and I glanced down to see a text from Judge Beck, asking where I was. Drat. My car was in the drive. He must have known that I'd taken Cagney out for a walk and was wondering whether to start dinner or not.

"Go on home," Suzette urged. "I'll call you later and let you know if I find out anything else. If that detective wants to talk to you again, he can go over to your house, or call and ask you to stop by the station. There's no sense in you staying here for hours."

I hesitated, wanting to go but not wanting to leave Suzette here with these two in her kitchen and half the police department outside. It wasn't fair that she'd had to deal with Travis almost drowning in her pond not three days ago, and now a dead man on her property.

"Is Olive coming over?" I asked, not wanting her to be alone tonight.

She nodded. "Olive is on her way. She just wanted to swing by her place and get an overnight bag. I'll be fine."

"Call me if you need anything," I told her. Then I got up and went to fetch Cagney from the upstairs bedroom where she and Gus were happily chewing on some peanut-butter stuffed dog toys. At the last minute I remembered the drone, and grabbed it off the kitchen counter before saying goodbye and heading home.

One block from my house I realized something. Miranda said she'd packed up and headed back to the office at noon, but I'd been at the Historical Society from one to two, and Miranda hadn't been there.

She'd lied about that. What else had she lied about?

CHAPTER 20

"I'm home!" I called out as I came through the front door and bent down to unsnap Cagney's leash. Taco was already in the house, grooming himself as he sat on the window seat. I felt a stab of guilt that the poor cat had probably been waiting on the porch for me to come back and feed him his dinner. Obviously someone had let the cat back inside, though. And clearly he'd been fed or he would have planted himself at my feet, telling me he was starving to death.

Cagney took off toward the kitchen and I followed her, setting the wet and muddy drone off to the side of the counter. The smell of pork loin and rosemary came from the oven. A pot of pasta boiled on the stove. Judge Beck was chopping vegetables for a salad. He had on a "kiss the cook" apron that the kids had gotten him for Christmas. I obeyed the apron and came up behind him, wrapping my arms around his waist and kissing him. I was aiming for his cheek, but with the angle, ended up smooching his jaw instead. Close enough.

"I didn't realize this dog was going to require marathon

training level walks." He turned and pulled me over to tuck me against his side for a quick hug.

"She's pretty energetic, but that wasn't what kept me so long." I told him about my visit with Suzette and the body I'd found on our walk, keeping my voice low so the kids couldn't hear. It was bad enough that a schoolmate had almost drowned on Friday without adding a death on top of the things they needed to process.

"Do you think it was an accident?" he asked. "I mean, Travis almost drowned in that pond three days ago. Maybe the man slipped on the icy mud, hit his head, and drowned."

I shrugged. "Maybe. Toots thinks it's murder. And he's convinced it was me, or Suzette, or maybe that neighbor who confronted the developer and the surveyor this morning with a shotgun. Honestly, I'm pretty sure Toots suspects everyone. We all might end up in jail."

The judge shot me a quizzical look. "Who is Toots? And what's this about a neighbor and a shotgun?"

I noticed he wasn't particularly bothered at the thought that I might end up in jail. Not that I was either, although with Toots on the case, who knew?

"He's a new detective with the county. And the neighbor is over on Broad street. The back of his property boarders Suzette's and there's some discrepancy about the boundary line. The surveyor hopped the guy's fence, and the home-owner threatened him with a shotgun."

"The surveyor who later is found dead, facedown in Suzette's pond?" Judge Beck's eyebrows rose. "I'm not a detective, but I believe this Toots should be questioning the neighbor with the shotgun and not pestering you and Suzette."

Huh. So maybe he *was* bothered about the detective suspecting me after all.

"The woman from the Historical Society did say she

heard what might have been a gunshot when she was leaving around noon," I commented.

The judge shrugged. "Sounds like this neighbor might have at the very least contributed to the surveyor's death."

"But I couldn't see any wounds on him that looked like they came from a shotgun. All I saw was a wound on the back of his head," I told the judge.

He thought about that for a second. "The neighbor shoots up in the air. The surveyor is scared that he's about to get a rear full of buckshot and takes off. He slips while he's running and falls, hitting his head and knocking him out. And he drowns. Or dies from the head wound."

It did make sense. Except… "The pond is pretty far from the back property line. Floyd Ambrose is in his eighties and doesn't look like he's in any condition to jump a fence and chase a guy across a field. So if it happened like you're proposing, the surveyor should have stopped running after a hundred yards, and not be still hauling butt when he came near the pond. Plus, why try to practically run *through* the pond? Why not go around it? By that point, he must have known that Ambrose wasn't after him."

The judge returned to the salad, tossing in the tomatoes and slicing the cucumbers. "Then it was probably just an accident. The guy was surveying, slipped or got stuck in the mud. Fell. Knocked himself out. Drowned. A horrible accident that just happened to have occurred three days after a rather similar accident."

"Maybe he was going in after the drone like Travis was," I said, half joking. "Cagney found it near where I found Stan. I brought it home thinking I might be able to look up the serial number. There has to be a registry or something for those things."

"There is. Drones have to be registered with the FAA and prominently display that registration number prior to flying." He shot me a quick glance, then continued slicing cucumbers. "But that doesn't mean everyone follows the rules. Not registering a drone comes with some pretty steep civil and criminal penalties, but no one is going to slap some twelve-year-old flying his Christmas present around with a fine, even though even cheaper toy drones are still required to be registered."

I walked over to the counter and picked the thing up, noting a serial number etched into the side, and a partially torn sticker on the top.

"I'd wanted to ask if it was illegal to fly these things over someone else's property. I mean, that's an invasion of privacy, right?"

"Not necessarily. Private property doesn't extend to the airways, which is why drones need to register with the FAA. They're considered mini aircraft, and it *is* legal to fly them over someone's property in this state. But there are nuisance laws and other laws that might come into play as well. If someone is using a drone to spy on someone, or perform an illegal activity, then they could still find themselves facing criminal or civil charges."

"So if someone was flying one over the backyard while I was sunbathing, I couldn't shoot it down?" I asked, only half serious. "Or use one of those jammers?"

"That's considered endangering an aircraft, believe it or not." He tossed the cucumbers in the salad. "The best course of action would be for you to contact the police and claim harassment. Drones are one of those weird gray areas where the law hasn't quite kept up with technology."

I nodded. "But I should be able to look up who this belongs to? And figure out why the heck they were flying it around Suzette's back property pre-dawn on Friday?"

He put the cutting board and knife in the sink, then

turned to face me. "You think this drone has something to do with the surveyor's death?"

I lifted one shoulder. "I don't know. Maybe. Maybe not. It could be that the surveyor's death was an accident, and the timing between that and Travis's near drowning is coincidental. Either way, I really want to know who owns this thing, and why they were snooping around Suzette's place."

He smiled before turning to pull the pasta off the stove. "You might end up being disappointed. It could be some kid up early for school and playing with a Christmas present, or some hobbyist neighbor who works third shift and was having some fun after work. I could absolutely see someone who didn't want to disturb neighbors by flying their drone around their backyard or up and down the street early morning might decide to fly it in what they thought was just an empty field."

I sighed, pulling the bottles of dressing from the fridge. "You're probably right. The owner is most likely too embarrassed to knock on Suzette's door to ask for it back, or maybe he didn't even see where it went down. And the surveyor's death is probably an accident, just like Travis's near drowning. There have just been so many murders this last year that I'm seeing crime around every corner."

I took the salad and dressing out to the table and called the kids down for dinner before heading back into the kitchen. The judge drained the pasta then tossed it with a pre-made pesto sauce, and I pulled the porkchops out of the oven. Henry and Madison came in to get the plates and silverware to set the table. The boy hesitated at the doorway, his gaze snagging on the drone.

"Oh, cool! Where'd that come from?"

"Cagney found it over at Suzette's when we were walking with her and Gus," I told him, not mentioning what else we'd found.

"Can I check it out later? Some of my friends have them, but that one looks different."

The judge glanced over at me and I nodded. It wasn't like the boy could damage the thing any more than three days in freezing water and mud had done, and I had other priorities for tonight. From what Judge Beck had said, flying it around Suzette's property wasn't a crime, so the drone would take a back burner to going over all the stuff from the Historical Society.

"You can mess with it, but only after you're done with your homework," the judge told his son. "Miss Kay is going to trace the registration number and return it to the rightful owner, so be very careful with it, okay?"

"Will do," Henry promised.

The kids set the table and helped put the food out. We all sat down for dinner and a discussion about the proposed fundraiser at Suzette's. I winced, thinking that I'd need to talk to her once more about that. After what happened with Stan, she might be less willing to have the community wandering around her property—especially if his death was a tragic accident. It seemed that once more Suzette might be giving more consideration toward selling the land for development than risking another injury or death on her property.

As the others talked, my mind wandered. Bernard Long was eager to get his hands on the land. Maybe he'd known Suzette was wavering and that another accident on her property would push her into making a hasty decision in his favor. He'd said the surveyor was a complainer. Maybe Long had come back and whacked Stan over the back of the head, getting rid of a problem employee and convincing Suzette to sell. Or maybe Floyd hadn't used his shotgun on the pesky surveyor. Maybe the elderly man was skilled with a slingshot and had killed Stan with a well-placed stone to the back of the head. If it had been the weapon David had used to kill Goliath, then a slingshot could have killed Stan. Or maybe Floyd had thrown a stone at him shot-put style, across several acres, and hit him hard enough to at least knock him out if not kill him.

Miranda had lied about going back to the office. Maybe she'd been the one who'd killed the man, although I couldn't for the life of me think of why.

Goodness. I was just as bad as Detective Toots, coming up with wild ideas of who might have murdered the surveyor, when the man's death was most likely an accident. Bernard Long had looked shocked and scared, and so had Miranda. It seemed extreme for the developer to kill his surveyor on the slim chance it might help him buy some land. And just because a woman lied about quitting early and going home, it didn't make her a murderer. And it was a real stretch to think that Floyd Ambrose was a champion shot-putter or slingshot shooter.

The kids got to work on the dishes after dinner. I fed Taco and Cagney, then settled in at the freshly wiped dining room table to get started on the stack of papers and booklets I'd brought back from the Historical Society.

The houses on our street had been built at the turn of the nineteenth century, and I'd found the survey done in 1898, right before building began. But that survey was just for the land that was sold and the houses on our street, so it didn't include the property line with the Millers. The Miller property that included Floyd Ambrose's house was sold off and surveyed in the 1960's. The last survey of that property line before 1960 was in 1858, so if there had been a handshake agreement between the Millers and the Hostenfelders, it would have occurred between 1858 and 1960.

Ugh. One hundred and two years of notes and correspondence would take me forever to look through, so I made some assumptions. Suzette's grandfather had been born in 1920, and her grandmother in 1926. I was sure if they'd made the agreement, that they would have said something to Suzette or her father at some point in their lives. That narrowed the window a bit. Figuring I'd start at 1858 and work my way forward, I settled in to start reading.

The contents of the booklets were a collection of diary entries and paperwork from the time of the Civil War. They were far more interesting than I'd expected and I soon found myself engrossed in the daily lives of the Miller family. I barely noticed the kids heading up to finish their homework, or the judge sitting across from me with his laptop and stacks of his own papers to peruse.

"These women baked more than I do," I muttered as I paged through the diary entries. The diaries didn't reveal the thoughts and feelings of the Miller women so much as they kept track of daily activities such as laundry, baking, church meetings, births, deaths, and illnesses.

"What the heck are you working on?" Judge Beck laughed. "Is there a murder-by-scone you're investigating? A recipe theft? Embezzlement at the donut shop?"

I leaned back and stretched my arms. "I'm reading the diary of one Gertrude Miller from 1860. There's a property dispute over Suzette's back boundary line. I'm trying to see if there's any record of a verbal sale or agreement between her family and the Millers that might shed some light on who actually owns that strip of land."

He chuckled. "Well I doubt Gertrude Miller was trading pies for some of the Hostenfelder land. Her husband would have been the one doing that, not her."

"The Millers would have been buying the land, not selling it, so technically Gertrude *could* have negotiated with the Hostenfelders," I told him. "And if her pies were really that good, then Elijah Hostenfelder might have cut a deal."

He shook his head. "She wasn't much of a businesswoman if she only wanted a ten-foot strip of land at the edge of a farm that belonged to her husband. There's not much she could have done with that small of a piece of property."

He was right, but this devil's advocate discussion was too much fun for me to let it rest.

"Maybe Elijah was trading a foot at a time, and Gertrude had hopes of eventually having enough for a small farm of her own." I glanced through my notes. "Elijah died in 1862. Maybe she only managed ten feet of land before he died."

The judge wiggled his eyebrows. "Maybe Gertrude was trading more to Elijah than pies for the land?"

Now I was the one who laughed. "Then she really was getting a bad bargain. Sex and pies for a tiny little strip of land? Plus Elijah was twenty and Gertrude was forty."

He grinned. "Elijah might have liked older women, and I'm sure Gertrude was a real looker well past forty."

I suddenly remembered the age gap between the judge and me and felt heat flood my cheeks.

"But she was married," I protested lamely, as if no one ever cheated on their spouse with an attractive, much younger neighbor.

"Well, if she wasn't trading pies and sex for land, perhaps you should be reading her husband's diary and not comparing your baking output to a woman from 1860," he teased.

"You make a valid point, Your Honor. Although I still would love to find a copy of this Walnut Jubilee Pie Gertrude made on March twenty-seventh." I set the booklet aside, figuring I could always come back to it later. And I could always inquire with the Historical Society to see if they had any of the Miller family recipes on record.

The other booklet was full of things like handwritten notes about the purchase of a mule, the sale of two steers, and several loan documents including extensions. It was a bit sad to see that the Miller family was already having financial trouble. Toward the end of the booklet, Gertrude's husband was selling off pieces of farm equipment and livestock, and I wondered how the family had managed to hold on until 1960 without selling the farm altogether.

It was midnight by the time I turned to the printouts. These were all letters from one of Gertrude and William's sons, Jerimiah, during the period in the Civil War when he'd served in the Union Army. There were also the replies that Jerimiah had saved from his mother, Orvil and Elijah Hostenfelder, and from his sister Julia. Since his father was still alive and running the farm, I doubted that Jerimiah would have been making deals to purchase a narrow strip of land from the Hostenfelders, but I became engrossed by the young man's account of army hardship and skirmishes, and once more found myself sidetracked.

At two Judge Beck stood and stretched. "I need to get to bed, and you should too unless you want to be half-asleep during your yoga tomorrow morning."

He was right. With a sigh I put the papers aside and went to bed. There was nothing in the documents that couldn't wait for later. Actually, there was nothing in the documents that shed any light on the disputed property boundary at all. It all truly was the search for a needle in a haystack and I didn't even have a magnet to help me.

* * *

ALL THROUGH MORNING yoga with Daisy, I kept thinking of Stan and the whole situation over at Suzette's. Deciding to satisfy my curiosity, I texted J.T. and Molly that I'd be in a little late today, then told Henry I'd take over his dog-walking shift this morning. Armed with a giant go-cup of coffee and my pup, I headed around the block and into the development where the Miller farm had once stood, turning down Broad Street.

I couldn't tell from the street-level where the old Miller house had once stood. Not that I could tell from Suzette's second story window either. The entire farm had been razed and the land leveled during the development, so there were no signs at all of what had once stood where the grid-layout of streets and neat houses on their square, level lots now were.

But Floyd Ambrose still had an old apple tree in his backyard, a remnant from the original Hostenfelder orchard.

Floyd Ambrose answered his door promptly at my knock, making a fuss over Cagney and inviting me in. I refused coffee, but sat down at his kitchen table while my dog took advantage of the man's hospitality and chewed on the steak bone he'd offered her. Mr. Ambrose's kitchen overlooked the backyard. The entire back of the house was dotted with double windows, and the kitchen table sat next to an enormous bow window with potted herbs lined up on the seat.

"Did you find anything out about the property line?" He asked as he sat across from me.

I shook my head. "The surveys at the courthouse disagree. I'm looking through older letters and documents from the two farming families, trying to see if there was some sort of informal agreement regarding that strip of land."

His jaw set. "Ten feet is nothing to that woman who owns the field, but it's a lot when it comes to my backyard. It's not like she's done anything with that back part of her land anyway. Why is she gonna try and take a chunk of my backyard from me? That land includes my apple tree. I love that tree."

"I don't think she's going to take your land," I said in a soothing voice. "Suzette Hostenfelder is a kind and generous woman. I'm sure you and the other neighbors will be able to come to an agreement that will make everyone happy, but in the meantime, I'm still researching."

Mr. Ambrose scowled. "I hope she doesn't take my land from me. This week has been a nightmare, let me tell you. First those people in my yard and at my fence line, then these accusations that a chunk of my backyard might not even be mine. Then some cops show up at my house just when I'm getting ready to go to bed last night, yelling at me and accusing me of killing someone. I haven't left my house all day. I haven't gone out other than to get my mail. How the heck was I supposed to have killed someone?"

I grimaced, thinking that Detective Toots needed to work on his social skills. And his investigative skills as well.

He glared out the window at the field beyond his fence line. "I guess one of those men from yesterday called the police and complained, because the one guy kept insisting I'd shot someone, then chased him around, and whacked him in the back of the head." Mr. Ambrose snorted. "Like I've been able to run in the last two decades. I can barely walk to the end of the block and back without needing to sit down, and they think I somehow chased some guy down and killed him? Stupid cops."

"That surveyor you confronted yesterday morning was found dead on the other side of that field adjoining your backyard at around five thirty," I told him. "I don't think you did it, but you do understand the police might want to question you, given that you had an altercation with the dead man early yesterday morning that involved you brandishing a firearm and threatening to shoot him.

"It was loaded with rock salt," Mr. Ambrose snapped.

"I know, I know. But the police still have a duty to investigate. A man died," I told him.

He hesitated at that. "And it was murder?"

"I don't know, but the police are treating it as a homicide. As they should until the medical examiner rules it either an accident or murder."

"Can't imagine why anyone would murder the guy," Mr. Ambrose admitted. "A few neighbors came out to talk to him because he came back and was walking around people's backyards, setting up his tripod and stuff. He didn't come back into my yard, but I saw lots of the neighbors talking to him. None of them seemed too happy, but they didn't threaten him, or look like they were arguing."

"You saw?" I frowned, realizing that of course Mr. Ambrose would have seen. He was here all day, and he'd just said he hadn't left his house aside from going to get the mail.

"I watched all day. Here. With my binoculars," he admitted.

I stood and went over to the bay window, looking out across Mr. Ambrose's backyard and the field. "From here? Or did you go upstairs and look out from one of those windows?"

A guilty expression flickered across his face. "Here. Except when they were leaving around three, I did go upstairs trying to see them again. There's a little hill in the middle of the field that blocks the view, so once they went past there, I couldn't see them anymore."

"Them?" I asked, confused.

"The surveyor guy and the woman." He motioned toward his back window. "The woman who was digging around the fence line."

"They left together?" I waited for his nod, thinking that this was a second thing Miranda had lied about. I could see her covering up that she'd ditched out on an afternoon of work. Maybe she'd lied because she was freaked out that she might have been the last person to talk to Stan before he'd died. But regardless of her motives, she was a liar. And that made me wonder….

"When was this?" I asked him.

He shrugged. "Around three forty-five or so. I remember because it was right about the time I put on my kettle for my four o'clock tea. She was digging, and found a metal box or something. Then the surveyor came up and started talking to her. They spoke for a few minutes, and left together. And that's the last time I saw either of them."

Three forty-five. She'd said she'd left at noon and gone back to the office, but Floyd had seen her here nearly four hours later.

I glanced over at Cagney who was happily munching on her bone, then pulled a small notepad out of my coat pocket.

"Tell me exactly what you saw throughout the day," I told Mr. Ambrose, thinking that I might be more than just a little late getting in to work today.

He recounted his entire day from beginning to end. When he'd finished, I looked at my watch, grimacing at the time. It was late. I needed to get to work. But there was one more thing I wanted to do before I left.

"Do you mind if I take a look in your backyard?" I asked. "And over the fence line?"

He shrugged. "I don't have a problem with that."

Cagney ran around the fenced yard, bringing sticks for Mr. Ambrose to throw while I poked around the old apple tree. It was right against the fence line, and just over on the other side, was a whole lot of holes and dug-up ground. Clambering over the fence, I squatted down and began pushing aside the loose dirt and rock with my hands. A shadowy figure materialized beside me, squatting down and pawing at the dirt with insubstantial hands. I held my breath for a second, but the ghost didn't acknowledge my presence, so I scooted over closer to him, eyeing the ground he'd dug up over a century ago.

There had been holes dug here and there around the property, but it was clear that Miranda had spent a lot of time and energy right here where the ghost was squatting, under this old apple tree. I pushed a pile of dirt aside next to where an open hole lay, and noticed some flaked off rusted bits of metal and a spot of white.

Thinking it might be a root or a bit of quartz, I picked it up, brushing the dirt from the object. That's when I realized that what I held wasn't a stone or a root at all.

It was a pearl. A gorgeous, six millimeter ivory-colored pearl with a gold clasp affixed to the top of the sphere.

CHAPTER 21

I lay on the floor of J.T.'s house, trying not to breathe. Being late to work had meant that instead of going in to the office, I'd needed to come straight here. For the dreaded video.

The dollar-store clothing I wore had been dramatically slashed, and I had ketchup all over my stomach as well as across a portion of J.T.'s carpet. My boss had fretted for nearly ten minutes, Googling whether he could get the ketchup stains out of his carpet or not before he'd agreed to the added embellishment. In the end, dramatic effect won over carpet stains.

"Kay, stop breathing," J.T. commanded.

"I'm trying, but I don't *actually* want to die," I responded before holding my breath once more.

"Roll it," I heard J.T. command. A few seconds later I heard Molly scream and had to fight to keep my eyes closed.

"Oh, Kay, she's dead! And my dog is gone!" Molly pronounced in the most scene-chewing dialog I'd ever heard. Oh well. It wasn't like anyone went to "Gator" Pierson's YouTube channel for the high quality acting.

"Cut."

I gulped a much-needed breath and waited for J.T.'s command before standing up. Assuming there would be no retakes, my part in this little production was over. I'd gotten the text to go straight to my boss's house, dressed in the cheap clothing he'd provided, and had just done an hour of scenes where I'd introduced "Daisy" and "Kay" to a variety of stuffed animals that were meant to represent both Lady and the puppies. Molly had offered to bring in Starsky, and J.T. could also have used Cagney as well as Lady for his film, but he didn't trust actual canines to hit their marks or perform as expected, so we were using stuffies instead.

"Am I done?" I didn't wait for the answer before wiping ketchup from my arm onto the tattered shirt.

"You're done," J.T. announced. "How are things going with those process service jobs?"

I practically had whiplash from the change in topics, but I was used to that sort of thing with J.T.

"I put the folders on your desk." I sighed. "I feel sorry for them, J.T."

He waved a finger at me. "It's not your place to feel sorry for them. They agreed to the terms and conditions of the credit card when they accepted the offer. Now it's up to the judge to feel sorry for them, not you."

J.T. was right, but that didn't make me feel any better.

"Can I count on the both of you for the fundraiser at Suzette's? We're going to have a planning meeting next week," I said, proving J.T. wasn't the only one who could segue at the speed of light.

"I'll organize a petting zoo," Molly chimed in. "My friend Kylie has baby lambs and goats, and I have another friend that can bring a mini pony."

"I'll help Daisy with tickets and keeping track of the

money?" J.T. made a face. "And I'll spread the word around to get people to attend."

I knew these events weren't his thing, but I knew he liked Suzette and wanted to help her. And I knew Daisy would give him a frosty shoulder if he didn't do something for the fundraiser. J.T. might not be the most civic-minded person in the town, but he'd do anything for Daisy.

Strange how love could change a person sometimes.

I went into J.T.'s bathroom and cleaned up, tossing the ketchup-stained and torn clothes into his tub and putting my own clothing back on. Then I left, shooting Molly a sympathetic glance. The girl gave me a thumbs-up, apparently not minding the break from the daily routine of skip-tracing.

I headed to the office, surprised to see Miles waiting for me.

"No muffins or scones today," I told him as I unlocked the door. "Between finding a dead man while walking my dog and staying up all night reading how many pies women baked each week in the mid-nineteenth century, I just didn't have time."

"I didn't come for pastries, although I wouldn't say no if you'd brought any in today. I came to talk. With you."

I shot Miles a questioning glance, a bit worried at his somber tone. "Everything okay with you and Violet?"

"Violet and I are fine. It's about last night." He waited until we were inside the office and the door was closed before continuing. "I'm not a detective, although I'd like to try for that promotion sometime in the future. But I've been on the scene for lots of crimes, and especially murders this past year. I...I don't like how Toots is going about this one, and I wondered if I could run some things by you in a confidential kind of way."

Miles's eyes were worried, his mouth in that thin, tight line that meant he was stressed.

"I'll make every effort to keep anything you say confidential," I told him. "But if I end up on the stand at a trial, or I'm being questioned in an official capacity, or if Judge Beck asks me a direct question about it, then I'll have to betray your confidence."

He nodded. "I wouldn't expect anything else, Kay."

"Then go ahead and sit down. I'll put on a pot of coffee while you talk."

Miles plopped down in my desk chair. I put my bag and purse on J.T.'s desk, and got started on the coffee.

"First, it's the scene. There's holes everywhere. Literally and figuratively. It looks like someone's been digging around the pond. There's holes other places on the property as well, but we didn't exactly look over the whole field."

I nodded. "Miranda, the woman from the Historical Society, has been out digging on Suzette's property, trying to find artifacts that might help with Suzette's grant applications. I don't' know if the surveyor was digging any holes, but he might have been. Then there's groundhogs."

"And that developer *might* have had someone out to do preliminary work for potential wells and septic systems," Miles added.

I hid a smile. "That's good thinking, but we're all on city water and sewer, so Bernard Long wouldn't have bothered paying for that kind of work."

"Oh." Miles narrowed his eyes and thought for a bit. "There was blood on the ground near where the body was found, but I didn't see anything on a rock like I would have expected if the man had hit his head. I could see some dirt and grit around the wound, though. That made me think he might have fallen and hit his head after all."

Miles *would* make a good detective, when he was ready for that exam.

"This is where you probably need to wait for the Medical

Examiner report and see what your techs have found," I told him. "Maybe the pond water washed some of the blood away from a rock, or the blood wasn't readily visible because of the mud. And if he was hit with something, then there might be droplets of blood splatter that flew out and into the surrounding brush. The dirt and grit could have been because he fell, or been transferred off a weapon, or washed up on the back of his head when he fell into the water."

He sighed. "You're right. So here's the deal. Toots thinks it's murder. He thinks it was Floyd Ambrose—the old guy who threatened the developer and the surveyor earlier that morning."

"I was there when that confrontation occurred." I sat down in Molly's chair and faced him, holding off on telling him what I'd learned from Floyd Ambrose this morning. "Do you think it's murder?"

He shrugged. "I really don't know, but if it was, I'm pretty sure it wasn't that Mr. Ambrose who did it."

"Why do you say that?" I felt the same, but I was eager to hear Miles's reasoning.

"That Historical Society lady said she heard a gunshot, and given what happened that morning, I'd have wanted to question Mr. Ambrose as well. But I couldn't see any evidence of a gunshot wound on the body. Admittedly, I didn't examine it closely and it was dark even with the lights, but all I saw was that head wound. And the body was pretty far from Mr. Ambrose's property line. We looked and there was no blood in the area of the property line. The techs set up more lights and went over the area carefully while I watched, and there was nothing. If a man was shot, there would have been blood. There wasn't any blood, *or* any shell casings."

"Hmmm," I replied, still holding off on admitting that I'd

already been by Floyd Ambrose's house and was convinced of the man's innocence.

"There's more," Miles added. "Mr. Ambrose lawyered right up when Toots interviewed him. Toots is trying to get a search warrant. He's having a little trouble because the judge wants to know why the key piece of evidence in Toot's request is the shotgun when the ME hasn't determined cause of death yet, and there are no visible gunshot wounds on the body."

"Uh huh," I said, silently applauding that judge.

"Toots is livid, says even if the surveyor wasn't shot, he was probably scared by the shotgun blast, and it contributed toward his death. I'm not sure the judge is going to buy it, but who knows." Miles shrugged again. "Anyway, I got curious, so I went around to all the neighbors on that street and down the adjoining one last night to see who was home three to four o'clock yesterday and if anyone heard a shotgun blast, or any sort of gunshot. I found six people who were home at that time, and none of them heard anything."

"Shotguns are pretty loud," I said. "Are you thinking that Miranda lied?" Which would be lie number four, so I wasn't particularly shocked.

"Either she lied or she was mistaken about the sound. She seemed pretty shaken by the whole thing, and I know how witnesses can get confused. I can't think of any reason she'd have to lie, but..."

"But?" I asked, pushing him to think through his reasoning.

"Time of death is a little bit of science and a lot of art, and it's not easy to pinpoint," Miles explained. "Still, I wonder if the surveyor didn't die right around the time that Miranda said she was leaving. She said she didn't talk to him, but he was found right where there were recent holes dug. She said she heard a gunshot that no one else in the neighborhood heard. She said she left early that day when she hadn't left early any other day according to Ms. Suzette."

"Do you think maybe she and the surveyor got into an argument? That she pushed him or hit him with a shovel in a panic because she thought he might get physical? And now she's freaked out because she didn't know he was dead and she'd left the scene?"

Miles nodded slowly. "That or she saw who killed the surveyor and is afraid the same thing might happen to her if she told."

"We were all talking about Mr. Ambrose and the shotgun at Suzette's table when she arrived. If she heard us, she might have thought that was the perfect misdirect."

Miles glared. "That's a horrible thing to do. Even if she was afraid, she implicated an old man who might be completely innocent."

"This is some good investigative work, Miles," I told him.

"Yeah, but there's no murder until the M.E. says there is. Plus I've still got Toots trying to get a search warrant and railroad an old man. I'm willing to bet ballistics on that shotgun is going to show it hasn't been fired in a decade. And the M.E. is going to come back and say that the surveyor slipped on some mud and hit his head and drowned while unconscious." Miles huffed out a breath. "Ambrose is probably going to sue the department for harassment, all because Toots is an idiot and we had to go hire someone ourselves rather than keep using the very capable detectives in Milford."

I sat down in Molly's chair. "So, do you want to hear what I learned last night and this morning?"

Mile's leaned back his eyes wide. "Heck yeah, I do!"

"First, I was at the Historical Society from one o'clock until two o'clock yesterday afternoon. Ann was the only one there. Miranda says she left at noon and went back to work, but she wasn't there when I was.

"So she lied." Miles frowned.

"She lied more than once. It turns out that Mr. Ambrose is a man with a lot of time on his hands and a raptor-like focus on what's happening right outside his backyard," I told the deputy. "After the altercation yesterday morning, he was concerned the surveyor would come back, so he spent the day at his kitchen window with a pair of binoculars, watching everything that happened in his backyard, and in the neighboring yards and Suzette's field. He saw the surveyor return shortly after the altercation. Stan avoided Mr. Ambrose's property as the developer had instructed, but he did shoot lines from the neighboring properties, which included climbing over some of those fences."

Miles took out his notepad, flipping through a few pages. "Those might have been the people I spoke to who were home yesterday. All of them said they'd seen a man working either on the other side of their fences, or in their backyard. A few went out to ask what he was doing, but most of them assumed it was some sort of utility work, and ignored him."

"It wasn't like Stan looked like someone who was casing their homes for robbery," I commented. "He was carrying surveyor's equipment. He was a thin, and non-threatening in his appearance. He was wearing clean but baggy clothing and a puffy parka."

"He didn't look like your stereotypical robber," Miles agreed.

I nodded. "By noon, Stan had moved on to another section of the property. Soon after, Mr. Ambrose saw a woman come up to the fence line who'd been there on Sunday, digging around. She was looking at a notebook as well as something on her phone, and carried a backpack as well as a shovel and a pick. Mr. Ambrose had gone out to talk to her the time before, and she'd agreed to stay on her side of the fence. Yesterday she continued digging around an old apple tree that's right on the property line as well as near Mr. Ambrose's fence."

Miles scribbled in his notepad. "That Historical Society woman, Miranda. We interviewed her."

"There's more," I told him. "Remember Miranda said she left at noon? That she'd only seen Stan from across the field and hadn't interacted with him? Well, as she was digging there just outside of Mr. Ambrose's yard, he saw her talking to Stan. Evidently they had a long conversation, then left together. Mr. Ambrose went upstairs and watched them walk through the field toward Suzette's house—toward the pond. He lost sight of them, but remembers it was a three forty-five."

Miles flipped through his notepad. "Between the time that Ms. Suzette arrived home, and what Mr. Ambrose saw, that would have been right close to the time Stan died."

"That was my thought," I agreed. "Maybe they parted ways and he slipped and fell, and she's lying because she's scared she'll somehow get blamed by your crazy detective. Or maybe she had something to do with Stan's death and is trying to cover it up. And then there's this." I pulled the pearl out of my pocket and sat it on my desk in front of Miles. "I'm sorry I probably ruined any fingerprints on it, but at the time I didn't really think about it being potential evidence."

Miles grabbed a tissue and used it to pick up the pearl. "Where did you find this?"

"Near the apple tree in Mr. Ambrose's yard. It was in a pile of dirt near one of the holes. Miranda had been digging there, so maybe she dropped it?"

He wrapped it in the tissue and handed it back to me. "I don't think it's evidence of anything, Kay. There's no crime if she dropped an earring there. Suzette gave her permission to dig, and that's what she was doing."

I stuck it back in my pocket, a little disappointed, but knowing he was right. The pearl might have tied her to the location, but that didn't mean anything. But something bothered me about the pearl, something I just couldn't put my finger on.

"She lied about when she left and talking to Stan, though. That changes things. I think we need to go back and talk to Mr. Ambrose," Miles said softly. "And Miranda as well."

"And other neighbors who might have seen her after the time when she'd said she'd left," I reminded him. "I'm going to warn you that Mr. Ambrose might not be open to talking to someone in uniform though. You all didn't make the best impression on him last night."

Miles grimaced. "Toots didn't make the best impression on him last night. But I'll give it a shot myself. Solo. It'll put me on Toot's bad side and get me in trouble for messing with an official investigation, but I'm still going to stop by and see if Mr. Ambrose will talk to me. I don't want Toots to screw this up, Kay."

"Neither do I," I told him.

CHAPTER 22

I worked late, making up for the time I'd missed on Monday and on Friday. When I got home, Henry was already out giving Cagney her evening walk, and Madison was in the kitchen with her father, pulling vegetables and chicken breasts out of the fridge.

Judge Beck took one look at me, and grabbed my shoulders, pivoting me around and steering me toward the parlor. "You look dead on your feet. Go take a nap and we'll call you when dinner is ready."

"You only got four hours of sleep last night as well," I protested. "And you made dinner last night. I feel like I'm slacking here."

"*I* did not get up at six in the morning to do yoga in the backyard with my friend then take the dog for a long walk even though it was Henry's morning," he countered. "And I'm not cooking dinner tonight, Madison is. She's making a stir fry. This is one of the benefits to having teenage children. They walk the dog, they cook, and they do dishes. Now nap, because I know you'll probably be up late again tonight working."

I eyed my bag that held the printouts from the Historical Society and my laptop, but Judge Beck followed my gaze and snatched it up.

"Oh no. Nap. I'm putting this in the corner of the dining room next to the sideboard. You're not touching it until after dinner."

I hid a smile, dropping down onto the couch. "Okay, but that goes for you too, Judge Beck. No work until after dinner."

He held up a hand. "I promise. I'm going to take care of Taco and set the table, and that's it. I'll wake you when dinner's ready."

With a stir fry, dinner would probably be ready in half an hour—which would normally be the perfect amount of time for a refreshing nap as long as I could actually go to sleep, that is. Determined to at least try, I lay down on the sofa, snugging a pillow under my head. The judge put an afghan over me, and surprisingly I was out before he'd even left the room.

* * *

I COVERED A YAWN, staring with bleary eyes at the letters. The nap had helped, but after dinner, I'd begun to feel myself fade once more. If I made it to midnight tonight, I'd be happy. Actually, if I made it to ten, I'd be happy.

"Are the tales of Gertrude's pies no longer interesting?" Judge Beck asked.

"Gertrude's pies were riveting, but I've moved on to Jerimiah Miller's correspondence during the Civil War." I yawned again. "There's nothing in here about the property line between the Millers and the Hostenfelders, but the letters *are* interesting. Did you know Jerimiah was at the Battle of Antietam? A few months after the battle he's writing about the scarcity of food and how they've been commandeering livestock and produce from the locals."

"That was common during the Revolutionary War as well," the judge commented. "Feeding an army on the move has always been a problem."

"They're paying the farmers for what they take, but sometimes it's pennies on the dollar, and, of course, it's in U.S. currency which some of them think will be worthless in the near future." I sighed. "Everything is in turmoil. Julia says in one of her letters to her brother that they've taken to hiding money and valuables just in case the fighting draws any closer. They purposely aren't telling servants or even other family members where the stuff is hidden, since they're worried they might get raided. It sounds like they're burying it—probably in the fields where freshly turned ground wouldn't be as suspect."

"I can't imagine going through that," the judge said. "Battles practically on your doorstep. Armies approaching. Family and friends on both sides of the conflict. I'd be worried as well, and not just about money and valuables. What if my farm got torched? My livestock taken by the army as well as my house being robbed."

"Those fears are real." I held out a page. "Jerimiah admits that he's raided some of the houses and farms along with others in his troop. His sister Julia was appalled, telling him that 'mother would never approve of this sinful stealing from others, no matter if they be the enemy or not.' And he's not the only one. There are some letters back and forth between him and Orvil Hostenfelder, and the both of them are talking about raids and where to hide their 'spoils of war.'"

"Raids?" Judge Beck frowned. "You mean they looted houses and farms? I take it Jerimiah Miller wasn't taking chickens for the troops' dinner, but valuables?"

I nodded. "Jewelry, and coin, from what he says in his

letters. No paper money, because by that point he and his family weren't sure who was going to end up on top of this conflict. He didn't have a way to conceal or transport artwork or vases or stuff, so he only took jewelry and coin."

"What did his commanding officers think about that?" the judge asked.

"Jerimiah didn't specifically say, but I get the impression by this point in the war, some officers were looking the other way as long as the offenses weren't too egregious. These troops had been risking their lives, and were hungry, dirty, and injured. The southern merchants were jacking up prices for anything they tried to honestly purchase. It seems that the robbing of the dead, or the occasional raid on a nearby farm—especially if it looked to be a wealthy family—was tolerated."

"I don't like it, but I can see how these things happen," the judge commented. "But what happened to the jewelry? I thought the Millers were struggling at this point. Was the loot Jerimiah brought home enough to keep their farm together until when they sold in 1960?"

"Here's where it gets weird." I paged through the documents. "Jerimiah Miller came home for two weeks in 1862, then returned to service. He died in June 14, 1863 at the second Battle of Winchester. Orvil Hostenfelder, who was the younger brother of Elijah, also served, although in a different unit than Jerimiah. He died shortly after at Gettysburg. In their earlier letters, Orvil says something about them hiding their loot where no one will find it, and that when they're home on leave, they can 'deposit the treasure with the harpies who will guard it with their very lives.' Jerimiah seems reluctant to do that, saying he'd rather have it closer to home, but that he admits the harpies would be excellent guardians for their treasure."

"Are you thinking that they brought the coins and jewelry

back, hid it with harpies, then went back to war?" the judge asked.

I nodded. "Yeah. Except I have no idea who these harpies are. Was that his and Orvil's nickname for some single elderly women living nearby? Or a convent of nuns? I can't see either of them handing a treasure over to an elderly women to guard, but maybe they hid it on the woman's property somewhere?"

"Maybe. I'd like to think even an army would spare a farm run by an old widow, or a convent. That *could* be a safe place to hide something until the war was over and they could retrieve it."

"Except neither of them lived to see the end of the war," I told him. "I'm thinking that the two of them were the only ones who knew where this treasure was hidden. And they might have died before they told anyone."

"Then the treasure might still be there, in a convent of nuns or a farm where an elderly group of women once lived."

I shrugged. "It may have been discovered ages ago when the Miller house was torn down or the ground plowed for new crops. There might be no treasure left to find, but I still wonder. If it is still out there, it would probably be worth a fortune."

"And how does this have anything to do with Suzette's property line or an unfortunate death on her property?" he asked.

I grimaced. "It has nothing to do with either of those. Honestly at this point I think Suzette is going to need to come to a negotiated agreement with the other property owners. As far as I can tell, there's nothing to indicate a handshake agreement over the moving of the property line, but I know Suzette won't want to take a hard stance about this. She'll want to be fair."

"Which is why we all love Suzette," he said. "But going

back to the looting and jewelry and coin, how many treasures lay hidden for over a century undiscovered? I don't believe there's much of a chance this loot is still out there somewhere, but it's fun to think there could be buried treasure somewhere nearby," Judge Beck commented.

"There are hidden Picassos and Rembrandts that come up now and then. There are archeologists who find buried treasure when excavating an old town or house. It could still be out there. Somewhere," I told him.

"A treasure. In the house of a harpy," he added. "Just waiting for someone to find it."

CHAPTER 23

I was in bed by midnight. A good six hours sleep plus my nap before dinner didn't quite leave me feeling completely rested, but I wasn't as exhausted as I had been the day before.

The cold snap had settled in overnight and there was a sparkling of frost on the ground. Daisy and I probably should have done our yoga downstairs in the rec room, but the dogs needed the outdoor exercise, so we bundled up and headed for the backyard.

"I've stayed up late reading those documents from the Historical Society for two nights now and haven't found anything that refers to the boundary line between the Hostenfelders and the Millers." I complained as I awkwardly attempted a cobra pose in my winter clothing. "Nothing. Absolutely zip."

"Well it was a long shot anyway," Daisy said.

"The last survey of Suzette's says she owns that ten foot strip, but the survey done in the '60's for the development of the Miller property shows them as owning it," I told her.

"Prior to that, the Miller property doesn't include that strip of land."

"Sounds like the surveyor for the developer made a mistake," Daisy said. "If it goes to court, the ruling is likely to be in Suzette's favor."

"She won't want to incur the expense of taking it to court for such a small strip of land," I said. "Plus she wouldn't want all the neighbors mad at her over ten feet she'd be taking from everyone's backyards."

"Then why did you bother going to all the trouble of reading these letters and diary entries?" Daisy laughed. "Sounds like Suzette made up her mind just from the courthouse research you did Monday afternoon."

"It was a silly idea," I agreed. "I just wanted to see if there was anything in writing, but it's unreasonable to expect to find what might only be a few sentences about a handshake agreement in over a hundred years' worth of documents." I smiled sheepishly. "I started out hoping to find some reference to a deal, but I'll admit I really stayed up for two nights reading because the letters and diaries are pretty interesting. Do you know Gertrude Miller used to bake over a dozen pies every Tuesday? And that there might be buried treasure somewhere?"

"Buried treasure?" Daisy exclaimed.

I noticed how she was more interested in the treasure than in the pies.

I laughed. "I'm sure it was found ages ago—if there ever really was a treasure, that is. In the letters during the Civil War, Jerimiah Miller and Orvil Hostenfelder had evidently crossed some ethical lines and looted. There had been talk back home about hiding valuables in case the fighting moved this way, and the guys were planning to hide their stolen goods as well when they were home on leave."

"Did they say where?" Daisy practically bounced with

excitement. "The Miller house was torn down almost a century ago, but maybe they hid it somewhere at Suzette's house? Or in one of the barns or outbuildings?"

"Suzette's house isn't very big, in case you haven't noticed," I reminded her. "And I'm sure her grandparents, her parents, and even Suzette know any hiding places in the cabin. As for outbuildings, most of those are long gone. Suzette's got that old barn and the chicken coop, but they're just post and frame. There's no hidey-hole I can think of in either of those."

"So they buried the treasure like proper pirates," Daisy speculated. "There's got to be a map somewhere with an X on it. Maybe it's under a big old oak, or out by the fence line."

"If they ever did get around to hiding the treasure, it's being guarded by harpies." I chuckled at Daisy's expression. "Seriously. That's what Orvil said in one of his letters. It made me think they hid the loot at the house of an old pair of maiden aunts in town, or maybe at a nunnery."

Daisy shook her head. "No, they'd want it close where they could see it or at least have an excuse to stroll by and check on it now and then."

"You're right. If it were me, I'd be constantly worried that someone might have stumbled upon my hiding place and taken my treasure. I'd want a good reason to see the spot regularly. So not a nunnery. And unless Orvil and Jerimiah visited their maiden aunts a few times a week, then probably not there either." I thought for a second. "Except Jerimiah and Orvil both went right back to the front lines after their leaves. They died on the battlefield. So neither of them would have been home to keep an eye on the buried treasure site."

"Their family would have, though," Daisy suggested.

I shook my head. "They wouldn't have known. Neither of the guys wanted their families to know they were looting.

Jerimiah Miller hinted about it to his sister Julia and she had a fit."

Daisy's arms dropped to her hips, the Mountain pose turning into something that I wasn't sure was yoga. "Then they definitely wouldn't have hid their treasures in either house.

I mirrored her position. "They may not have hidden it at all, or even had it when they returned from leave. From what I can see, they were only here for a few weeks, overlapping each other's visit by three days. I'm betting if they still had the treasure, they would have buried it and kept the location secret aside from telling each other. They were both returning to battle. They must have known there was a chance one of them wouldn't come back and they'd want the other to know where the treasure was."

"Only neither of them came back," Daisy said, her voice sad. "Do you really think they had the loot? And that they brought it home to hide while they were on leave?"

I shrugged. "From the letters, it's pretty clear that Jerimiah did steal from some of the farms as well as dead Confederate soldiers, and I got the impression Orvil had as well. So they were in possession of treasure at one time. If their commanding officer had discovered it, they would probably have been disciplined and none of that shows up on any of the letters or the official documents about their service."

"Maybe the commanding officer was dirty," Daisy suggested. "Maybe when he found out, he confiscated it and kept it for himself, which would mean he'd not want to be reprimanding the offender or have any sort of official document about the looting. It's also a possibility one of his fellow soldiers found out about it and stole the goods."

I nodded. "Definitely a possibility. But with those sorts of risks, the guys would absolutely have wanted to hide the loot here when they were on leave rather than continue carrying it around with them on the battle field."

Daisy nodded, growing excited once more. "We should talk to Suzette and see if she has any ideas about where they might have hidden the treasures. Then we should start digging. If any of this is truly valuable, it might help pay for all of Suzette's repairs and the pond restoration."

Start digging. I frowned. I knew next to nothing about archeology, but Miranda had been digging in some weird spots around Suzette's. Her excavations weren't the careful layer-by-layer gridwork I'd seen in shows and in museum photos. She dug holes in one place, then went somewhere else. Like she was looking for something specific—something she thought might be along Suzette's back property line or along the pond edge.

"Miranda scanned all these letters and documents into the Historical Society system," I thought out loud. "She's a history buff. If I came to these conclusions, then she would have as well. No wonder she was so eager to dig around on Suzette's property under the guise of finding items to help Suzette with her grant applications."

Daisy's eyebrows shot up. "You think she wants to find the treasure and keep it for herself? Not tell Suzette?"

That was exactly what I thought but once Daisy had said it, the guilt settled in. "Maybe she just wants the credit for finding the treasure? And maybe she truly is hoping to find it and help Suzette restore the property. She is a historian. Those might be her motivations. I don't know. This could just be wild imagination on my part, but she lied about when she left on Monday. She lied about her interactions with Stan that day. And Floyd Ambrose did say he saw her walking away with a metal box. It makes me wonder if she found the treasure—or at least one of the treasures. And if she did, she certainly didn't mention it to anyone."

I frowned, remembering the pearl. What if it hadn't been an earring or something Miranda had been wearing that she'd dropped. What if it had come from the box, and had fallen out?

Daisy snorted, interrupting my thoughts. "Kay, your gut is usually right. And I'm getting the impression your gut is saying Miranda is a thief and maybe a murderer."

I frowned. "Maybe or maybe not. Maybe she hasn't found anything but nails, hinges, farming tools, a bent frying pan—stuff like that."

"That's all she's *told* Suzette she's found." Daisy gave me a look full of significance. "What if she found the treasure, just dumped a bunch of junk on Suzette's counter, and took the valuable stuff home."

"Then why keep coming back to dig?" I asked. "Suzette mentioned she was there Tuesday."

"Because there's two treasures to find? Or because she wants to keep up her cover of looking for artifacts for Suzette's grant application?" Daisy added.

I wanted to roll my eyes, but there did seem to be a whole lot of puzzle pieces fitting together here. Miranda had been the one who'd scanned the letters for the Historical Society. She was the one digging at Suzette's property. She'd lied several times when it seemed like she should have had no reason to lie.

She was there when the surveyor died. They were seen talking to each other right about the time he would have died. Maybe she was there when it happened. Maybe she'd killed him.

And I was falling down that hole once more. I had no proof of any of this. Heck, for all anyone knew, the surveyor's death had been a complete accident.

Our yoga session finished, Daisy and I rounded up the dogs and went into the house for our coffee. I put out a box of store-bought donuts the judge had brought home last night, and offered one to Daisy, apologizing that I hadn't made anything since Sunday's muffins which had been gobbled up Monday.

"Hey, donuts look good to me," Daisy said, taking a cruller. "Not as good as your baked goods, but still tasty."

"I'm nothing compared to Gertrude Miller," I told her. "The woman made twelve pies every Tuesday. Every. Tuesday."

"Yes, you told me." Daisy shoved the crueler into her mouth, trying and failing to hide her smile.

"You may laugh, but I'm on the hunt for her Walnut Jubilee Pie recipe. It sounds amazing."

"I'll totally taste test that one," Daisy promised.

"Taste test what?" Henry asked as he shuffled into the kitchen. The boy was wearing plaid fleecy pajamas and a T-shirt, looking like a younger, shorter, and darker-haired version of his father.

"Walnut Jubilee Pie," I told him. "A woman wrote in her diary from back before the Civil War that it was a family favorite."

Henry wrinkled his nose. "I'm not a big fan of walnuts." He reached for a chocolate-iced cake donut. "But I *am* a big fan of these."

"Me too," Daisy told him.

The boy shoved the donut into his mouth and took the milk out of the fridge. Before pouring it, he hesitated and removed the donut from his mouth.

"Oh, Miss Kay! I forgot to tell you that I took a look at your drone. It's made by a company called Robotic Integrations Inc. That particular model has a metal detector built in and as well as a night-vision camera. Super cool."

"Super cool," I agreed, thinking that might be why the owner had been flying it around pre-dawn. A night-vision camera wouldn't produce the most artistic pictures, but they at least would be visible. And a metal detector?

"I tried to look up the registration number, but evidently only cops can access that stuff, so I e-mailed the Robotic Integrations people and gave them the serial number, figuring if someone spent that much money for a drone, they would have registered it. They said they couldn't give out customer information, but that they'd be happy to contact the customer and let them know that we found their drone. So I gave them your phone number and e-mail address."

"Good thinking," I told him.

"You found the drone?" Daisy asked.

Drat. With everything that had been going on, I'd forgotten to tell her about that.

"Technically Cagney found the drone," I told her. And then five seconds later, I had found Stan-the-Surveyor's body.

Near the drone. And I'd fallen because I'd stepped in a hole—a hole that had been freshly dug. Once more, Miranda seemed to be right in the middle of everything that was occurring here. I thought about the drone, a metal detecting drone when everything Miranda had found when digging had been metal. Maybe she hadn't waited for the perfect opportunity to dig on Suzette's property. Maybe she'd flown a drone around, trying to find the spots to dig, planning on doing it under cover of darkness, but had lost the drone. Then when Suzette had called the Historical Society asking about potential grants, she'd found a second chance to search for the treasure.

I shook my head to clear it of those thoughts. This was all wild conjecture. No crime had been committed by flying the drone over Suzette's property. Miranda was currently digging there with the permission of the owner, and I had no proof at all that she'd found anything she hadn't given to Suzette.

Except maybe that pearl.

But as of right now, I couldn't connect her to any crime. While I might suspect Miranda's ethics, so far I couldn't see that she'd done anything wrong.

But I sure hoped that drone manufacturer put me in contact with the owner of the drone. And I hoped the owner wasn't who I thought it was.

J told Madison that I'd take over walking Cagney this morning, realizing that this would be three days in a row I'd taken on this task. It was nice, following up morning yoga with a long walk, but I didn't want to make a habit of this. Judge Beck was right. The kids needed to take responsibility for Cagney's care, and that included her walks.

But for today, as yesterday, I had an ulterior motive.

I first headed down toward Suzette's house, walking down her driveway and around the side yard to look at the pond and across the field.

Suzette had put Travis's bike into a neighbor's garage for safekeeping, but I went to where the boy had left it, then looked once more, trying to see things from what would have been his vantage point. From the corner of the house the pond and the back field looked like a giant mess of tall weeds, bushes, and scattered saplings. The crumbled dock was on the left of the pond and I could see the sun glinting off the thin ice of the water. On the right side of the field, close to the backyard, was the old chicken coop, and about fifty yards farther into the field stood a small dilapidated barn. From here, I couldn't see the row of houses that lined Suzette's back property line, but I could see the faint curl of smoke that was clearly coming from someone's chimney. With the weeds, brush, and the slight curve of the land, it looked like the field went on forever.

The back door of the cabin opened. "Kay? Oh my gosh, you gave me a start. What are you doing out here?"

Cagney jumped at the end of her leash, straining to reach Suzette.

"I'm so sorry," I said. "I thought you'd be at work. I just wanted to check a few theories before I headed in myself."

"I took the day off." She blew out a breath. "I hope I don't end up getting fired over all this, but I'm pretty sure finding a dead man in your backyard is a good excuse for a day of sick leave."

"It is in my book," I told her, even though I didn't intend on taking the day off. Unlike Suzette, I'd seen more than one body in the last year, and although the experience still shook me, I sadly seemed to be getting used to it.

"Since you're here, do you think I could go upstairs and look out your back windows?" I asked, figuring I might as well look at everything from a higher vantage point as well.

"Sure." She opened the door wide, and Cagney and I walked in.

"Do you need more coffee?" Suzette asked, eyeing my go-cup.

I held it up and wiggled it. "I just filled it, thanks."

"Then come with me." Suzette led the way up a steep set of narrow stairs, the wooden treads worn in the middle from centuries of footsteps.

The second floor of the cabin had once been one large loft space, a bedroom that all the children shared. Sometime in the last century, it had been divided and framed out, providing two small bedrooms, a tiny full bathroom, and a small loft space where Suzette had put a chair and an end table. She opened a bedroom door, apologizing for the mess, and we went inside.

The room was barely large enough for the wrought iron bed and the walnut stained dresser, but it was cozy and inviting with a colorful quilt at the end of the bed and water-color rural landscapes on the walls. The small table beside the bed was stacked high with books, and a pair of slippers peeked out from the lacy dust ruffle. I tried not to be nosy, and went over to the windows that looked out over the back field.

The pond appeared an oval of weed-choked ice from here. The banks were not clean edges, the icy bits spreading into brush and briars, and covering half of the partially submerged dock. From here I could see the holes in the barn roof, and the roofline of the houses on the other side of the field.

"What are you looking for?" Suzette asked as she stood beside me scanning the landscape.

"I'm not really sure. The old Miller house would have been where?" I asked.

"There." She pointed off to the end of the field. "About three blocks into that development. My grandfather said you could see it from here when he was little. The Hostenfelders stubbornly refused to add on to this house, but other families tore down the original homes and rebuilt larger and more ornate ones over the years. The original Miller farmhouse used to be close to the property line, right at the edge of where the apple orchard was. It was demolished around 1850, leaving some of the foundation there until the current development went in. In 1850, the Millers had built a large three-story home farther from the property line, but granddad said you could still see the top story, even with the dip in the land."

"If you were living here during the Civil War and wanted to hide valuables, to keep them safe from any raiding soldiers, where would you put them?" I asked.

Suzette shrugged. "I'd assume a raiding party would search the house, and probably even bunker down in the barn. They'd probably go through the chicken coop for eggs and meat as well. I know it sounds crazy, but I'd probably bury it in the manure pile."

I laughed. "Sounds like a perfect place to me."

"Or out in the field somewhere," Suzette continued. "If the soil was turned, then I'd bury it among the crops. Or under a newly-planted apple tree, if I wanted to hide it in the orchard."

Apple trees. I looked once more across the field, trying to envision three acres of trees, loaded down with fruit. There still was that apple tree in Mr. Ambrose's yard right on his fence line—the tree Miranda had been digging near.

The tree where she'd supposedly found a metal box. The tree where I'd found one lone pearl.

Orvil had suggested keeping their treasure where the harpies could guard it, but Jerimiah had wanted it close to home, where he could see the spot. Suzette was right. It would have been less safe burying it near the house, but home could mean different things to different people. Jerimiah would have been a child when the new Miller house was built and the original one demolished. Maybe home was the site of the old house, near the apple trees, a spot where he could see from the new house and where Orvil could see from this second story window.

Had Miranda come to the same conclusions? Was that why she was digging near the Ambrose property?

"How about you?" Suzette asked. "Where would you bury your treasure?"

I frowned, still thinking about what the demolished foundation of the old Miller house would have looked like in the mid nineteenth century.

"With the harpies," I replied distractedly.

Suzette burst out laughing. "Well, that's certainly a safe place for any treasure, except the harpies are long gone. We haven't had any here in mine or my parent's lifetime."

I turned to her, confused. "What? What do you mean? You used to have harpies?"

She smiled. "Of course. That's what our family always called the geese. Have you ever met a goose? They're noisy, aggressive, and insanely protective of their nesting spot. Harpies. The old nesting box on the other side of the pond would have been an ideal spot to hide something. Any raiding party wouldn't bother fierce geese, especially when there is a coop full of chickens and eggs not a hundred feet away."

Harpies. I looked out at the pond, squinting as I tried to make out where the nesting box had once been.

"The remains of it might still be there. Somewhere," Suzette said, also looking toward the pond. "The bank has shifted and moved over the years, so it's probably rotted and half underwater at this point, if there's anything left that is."

"Do you know where it was?" I asked her.

She nodded. "Not far from where you stumbled across that surveyor's body yesterday. Right around where I found Travis in the water."

"Right where Cagney found the drone," I mused.

She nodded. "Yep. And you're right. If I had a treasure to bury a hundred years or so ago, that would have been the ideal spot."

We headed downstairs, Cagney happily dancing around the living room as if we'd been gone for hours.

"One more thing," I asked Suzette before I left. "When you came home Monday, you said that Miranda wasn't here when you arrived. She didn't leave you anything? She didn't text you or say anything about what she found that day when she was digging? Like maybe a metal box?"

Suzette shook her head. "No. She texted that she left early because she hadn't had any success."

I thought about that a second. "When did you get the text?"

Suzette pulled her phone out and looked at it. "Just before four. Yeah, that's right. I was just pulling into the driveway when I got the message. She said she left around noon."

"She texted you at four that she left that day around noon —four hours earlier," I thought out loud.

"Yeah. I didn't really think about that at the time. I guess I figured she was just getting around to texting me, knowing I'd be home soon and expecting to see her. And no, she didn't have anything for me on Monday. She did have a few more nails and hinges yesterday, but nothing important. Honestly, I don't know why the woman keeps coming out here. She's not finding anything of value, and it can't be all that exciting to spend days digging in a weed-choked field. It's been three days now. You'd think she would have given up by now when all she's come up with is nails, hinges, and other bits of junk metal."

"Yeah," I said softly. "You'd think she would have given up by now."

CHAPTER 25

Miles stared forlornly at the empty space in front of the coffee maker.

"You know, it wouldn't hurt *you* to make us some baked goods now and then," Molly scolded him. "Or at least run by the bakery and pick something up. Heck, I'd even take a box of waxy-chocolate convenience store donuts as a reasonable attempt to pay us back for all the pastries you've eaten in the past few months."

"Who is this 'us' thing?" I teased. "I don't see you baking muffins and bringing them in to work. And Miles *did* bring us lunch on Friday. Remember?"

Molly held up her hands. "I'm not a baker. Or a cooker. Or really an anything-er when it comes to food. I have also sprung for lunch though, and I've brought in bakery-bought cakes on occasion."

Miles looked so chagrined that I took pity on him.

"It's okay," I told him. "I like you stopping by here, and I'm happy to trade baked goods for information you're not supposed to give me on various cases."

Ugh, now he looked even more sad. "I do have information. And I was hoping scones or muffins, or even store-bought donuts."

"I promise I'll make some scones tonight," I told him. "Your pick. You tell me your favorite and I'll make sure they're here for you tomorrow."

He brightened at that. "The espresso chip ones? No, the dried cherry vanilla. Those are my absolute favorite."

"Done."

He eyed the empty space again and sighed. "Not that I have any good news for you today anyway. Toots got his search warrant. Ballistics has the shotgun and the techs have pretty much the entire contents of the Floyd Ambrose's garage."

"He got his warrant?" I scowled, thinking that Judge Beck must not have been the one signing warrants this week, since I doubted he would have approved that one.

Miles nodded. "Cause of death is in, although we're still waiting for the toxicology screening and some of the other data. Basically Stan suffered a blow to the back of the head, and not from a fall. It was a blunt force trauma strike. He got knocked out, went facedown in the pond water, and drowned. The M.E. says the head wound is serious enough that he might have died anyway if he hadn't received immediate medical attention."

"Oh no," Molly breathed. "That's horrible."

And it was equally disturbing that a murderer had been on Suzette's property. By the pond. Once more my mind wandered to Miranda, the only other person who had been there. Could she have killed Stan? Was she even capable of such a thing? Suspecting someone of skimming found treasure wasn't the same as suspecting them of murder.

"It is. And the foul-play preliminary report was enough for Toots to get his warrant," Miles told us.

My heart skipped a beat. "So Floyd Ambrose is under arrest?"

"Not yet." Miles looked heavenward. "Even Toots isn't foolish enough to push for charges until we get more back on the evidence."

"But Stan didn't die from a shotgun blast," I argued. "And unless Mr. Ambrose was shooting cannon balls from his property clear across to Suzette's pond, I can't see how he could have killed Stan."

Miles lifted his hands. "I've given up trying to figure out how Toots's mind works. We didn't find any cannonballs or anything that could be the weapon at the scene of the crime. That's why I'm guessing we have every rake, shovel, and tire iron from Mr. Ambrose's garage in our tech lab."

Shovel. For digging. Suspicion gnawed at me, but what my gut was telling me would never be enough for an arrest. It was all flimsy, and ridiculously circumstantial.

"Your detective thinks a two-hundred-year-old man got angry at the surveyor, grabbed a tire iron, then ran through acres of weeds and into the mud and brambles around a half-frozen pond, bashed the surveyor over the head, then walked on home, had a cup of tea and watched some Matlock reruns?" Molly asked.

"I'm guessing that's exactly what he's thinking," Miles grumbled. "And Floyd Ambrose is eighty-five. I'm not saying he ran through three acres of weeds, but he might have been able to walk there. Slowly."

"Then walk slowly back after he killed the surveyor?" Molly rolled her eyes.

"She has a point," I told Miles. "Miranda—that woman from the Historical Society—was there. She was seen with Stan. She was seen walking back with Stan about the time of the murder. She lied about when she'd left. She'd lied about talking to Stan.

In addition the developer said his surveyor complained about several neighbors approaching him while he was working, and Mr. Ambrose confirmed that. Someone surely would have seen an elderly man slowly making his way through the field. Floyd Ambrose spent most of the day watching the goings-on through his binoculars. He saw Miranda and Stan talking around three forty-five. They walked back through the field together. Suzette got home at four. That only leaves a window of fifteen minutes. That's a pretty tight time window for Mr. Ambrose to grab a shovel, shuffle his way through a field of weeds looking for the surveyor, kill him, then make his way back before Suzette arrived home."

"Maybe one of the other neighbors was mad at the surveyor as well," Molly suggested. "A younger, fitter neighbor."

I shook my head. "It just doesn't sound right. Killing someone over trespassing when you could just call the police or chase them off? And Stan was killed next to the pond. That's not near any of the property lines. No one else should have been in that area except Suzette or Miranda."

"It's definitely not Suzette. So Miranda must be the murderer," Molly announced. "There. Case closed. Go arrest her, Miles. What are you still doing here? Go lock that woman up."

Miles scowled at the teasing. "Opportunity isn't enough to arrest someone. There's no motive. There's no means."

"She was using a shovel to dig around Suzette's place," I told him. "That's means. And she lied about when she was leaving the property as well as her talking to Stan. As for motive…I've got a weird long shot theory. I don't know if it's enough of a motive to kill someone, but if our only other suspect is an elderly man with a shotgun, then I think we do need to consider Miranda."

Miles was suddenly all cop, his attention laser focused on

me. "What do you mean she has motive? Did she know him beforehand? Spurned lover? Long-term feud?"

"Greed." I squirmed a bit, feeling like this was such a stretch, but needing to put it out there. "I've been digging around documents that the Historical Society has from the Miller family—old letters and diaries and stuff. I was trying to see if there was an informal agreement about the boundary line between what used to be their farm and Suzettes, and I couldn't find anything. But I did find some letters from Jerimiah Miller. He served in the Civil War and mentioned looting and wanting a safe place to hide his treasures when he came back briefly on leave. He and Orvil Hostenfelder both supposedly hid stolen valuables somewhere. They both died shortly after that in battle, and I don't see anything that says the treasure was ever located. Although, to be honest, it might have been found by someone who wanted to keep it a secret so they wouldn't be questioned or forced to give it back to the rightful owner."

"Buried treasure?" Molly laughed. "That's cool. I mean, it's not cool that someone stole, but I love the idea that there are hidden valuables somewhere in Locust Point."

"The Miller property was developed and their house torn down," I told her. "If it had been hidden in the house, I'm thinking it would have been found. But if the loot had been hidden somewhere on Suzette's property or near the property line, then it still might be there."

Miles shot me a skeptical look. "So how does Miranda come into all this, and why is buried treasure a motive for murder."

Here's where it all got dicey—as if the whole buried treasure thing wasn't dicey enough.

"She's been digging all over Suzette's property, supposedly looking for antiquities to help with Suzette's grant application. All she's found are a few nails and some other junk, but she keeps coming back every day and spending the whole day there, digging. She's the one who scanned these letters into the Historical Society computers. She has to know there might be treasure out there, and I think she's looking for it under the guise of helping Suzette."

"So why kill Stan?" Miles asked. "She's got permission to dig there. And until she finds and steals something, she hasn't committed a crime. If Stan came across her digging, he'd just shrug it off as that Historical Society woman doing what Suzette gave her permission to do. There's no reason for her to kill Stan."

"There is," I insisted. "According to Mr. Ambrose, she'd found a metal box and holding it when Stan approached her. The two talked, then walked back together. What if she and Stan had a deal to split the treasure—a deal they'd worked out either beforehand or at the time she found the box? What if once she realized what was in the box, she decided to cut her partner out of the equation, and whacked him over the head with her shovel?"

Miles blew out a breath. "Then why come back? She's found the treasure. Surely it's too risky to keep digging on the property after killing her partner—especially since she's found what she wanted."

"There are two treasures," I told him. "Orvil's and Jerimiah's. It sounds as if they hid them separately. What if Miranda had found one of the treasures, and Stan came across her when she was checking it all out? He sees her kneeling over a box full of gold coins and jewelry, and gets excited. He tells her he wants a cut or threatens to tell. So she agrees, walks back with him to a place where no one can see, then whacks him in the back of the head with her shovel, takes the loot and runs."

Miles frowned. "We did find some holes near the body that had been dug fairly recently—that I could tell, anyway.

And there was quite a bit of trampled briars and bushes, but I figured you and Cagney, and Stan might have done all that. It was muddy and slick, but I wonder if any of the techs pulled a decent shoe print that won't match to you or the dead man? Or if they found something else incriminating?"

"MIranda told us she left the property around noon, and that's when she heard a gunshot, but Mr. Ambrose saw her digging near his backyard after that point. According to him, she was there for several hours, not leaving until close to three forty-five," I pointed out. "None of the other neighbors heard a gunshot. And the window of time between Mr. Ambrose seeing her leaving and Suzette getting home is really small. It has to be her. Either Miranda killed him, or she witnessed who did."

Miles frowned. "The time window isn't enough to make her more than a person of interest. And she could just say that Ambrose is lying. Or senile. It comes down to who is more believable, and I'm going to tell you right now that a jury might believe a young woman who works for a nonprofit and is deep into research of local history over an elderly man who threatened someone with a shotgun in front of witnesses."

"True," Molly admitted. "But I think she did it."

"I think so too," I told him. "I just don't have quite enough evidence to prove it at this point. The two left," I counted off on my fingers. "Miranda and Stan. Together. At around three forty-five in the afternoon. And I'm pretty sure if you ask the neighbors, someone besides Floyd Ambrose had to have seen them. Miranda was carrying the box as she and Stan walked through the field toward Suzette's house. Mr. Ambrose lost sight of them as they crested a hill in the field."

Miles frowned. "Maybe the metal box held digging tools from her backpack or a metal detector. She had permission to dig there. And there's no crime in talking to someone else working the property or walking back to the house with him, even if it is suspiciously close to the man's time of death."

"But what about the pearl?" I took it out of my pocket and unwrapped it from the tissue. "I thought it was an earring or something she'd dropped, but what if it's old? What if it's part of the Civil War loot and it fell out of the box?"

"How would she not have noticed this pearl falling out of the box?" Molly asked. "Unless the box had completely fallen apart and this was just sitting in the dirt."

"From what Mr. Ambrose told me, I believe the box was intact. But Stan might have startled her when she was looking through the contents. Maybe she didn't notice this pearl had fallen out," I said.

"I could see that," Molly admitted. "A box full of old jewelry and coin, and trying to hide the contents from the surveyor. She might not have noticed that it had fallen out of the box."

"There's more," I told them both. "Cagney found the drone that Travis was looking for when he broke through the pond ice. Henry looked up a bunch of information on it via the internet, and left a message with the company that made it. They're going to pass on my contact information to the owner, letting them know that I found the drone and that I want to return it to its owner."

"But if it's Miranda's drone, she won't want it traced back to her," Molly warned. "She won't contact you to claim it."

"Then someone would need to get a warrant to get the owner's information from the manufacturer," I said, giving Miles a significant glance.

He sighed. "I'll come over to your house tonight to bag and tag the drone. I don't think Toots is going to make the connection between the drone, Travis, and the murder, but maybe I can do some stuff unofficially behind the scenes to find out more information. The manufacturer might not talk to you about the owner, but they might talk to me even without a warrant."

"Thanks, Miles." I smiled. "And if I find anything else out, I'll call you. And I'm definitely going to have those scones for you tomorrow morning."

He grinned and left. Molly and I returned to our work, with J.T. popping in and out throughout the day. Just as I was thinking of wrapping things up and taking a little work home with me, my cell phone rang.

I dug it out of my bag, and answered with a tentative "Hello," not recognizing the number.

"Mrs. Carrera?" A perplexed voice asked. "This is Ann down at the Locust Point Historical Society."

"Hi Ann." I wasn't sure why she was calling me. Maybe she'd come up with more documents for me to buy about the Miller and Hostenfelder property line.

Or maybe she was calling me about something Cagney had found in Suzette's pond Monday night.

"I apologize in advance for calling you like this, but I got an e-mail that said you have our drone?" She laughed, and it was a strained, tense sound. "I figured that couldn't be right because we haven't taken it out of the safe in the last few months, but I went and checked and it's gone. Where did you find it?"

And just like that, another piece of the puzzle snapped in place. Now all I needed was that pesky thing called proof.

CHAPTER 26

"Ijust don't understand it," Ann told me. "When I got the e-mail from the manufacturer, I thought they must be mistaken. But it's not in the cabinet. And it's not signed out by anyone either."

"Is the cabinet locked?" I asked.

Ann nodded. "Although everyone knows where the key is. We keep all sorts of things in there—cameras, and metal detectors mostly. That drone was a donation from a local historian and reenactor, Dr. Potilla. It's worth almost a thousand dollars, but given all the valuable items we have in the museum as well as our computer equipment, it's an odd thing for someone to steal."

"They didn't steal it to sell it," I told her. "They stole it to use. Whoever had it was flying it around Suzette Hostenfelder's back field last Friday. They must have been piloting it from a distance, because when the paperboy came by, he didn't see anyone around. He did see the light from the drone, though. And he saw it go down."

Ann shook her head, her expression puzzled. "The drone has a camera and a metal detector on it. We use it when we're going over a large amount of land like a battlefield. Maybe the person who stole it is a history buff and was trying to find souvenirs? But why Ms. Hostenfelder's property? There wasn't a battle anywhere near that farm. The most they'd probably find was random household goods—things like nails, rusted hinges, or an old horseshoe."

"Who has access to the key and knows about the drone?" I asked, postponing the "why" for later.

Ann held up her fingers one at a time. "Me. Miranda. Our six volunteers."

"And how long has Miranda worked at the Historical Society?" I asked.

She frowned. "Three years. But there'd be no reason for her to steal the drone. All she had to do was tell me and sign it out. She's quite the historian and very dedicated to our little museum. I was a bit surprised when she accepted the offer, because we don't pay much, but her mother was a Miller, and she was thrilled to have the opportunity to work on documents and letters that relate to her family history."

My mouth dropped open. "Miranda is a Miller?"

"On her mother's side. Her great grandparents were the ones who sold the farm to development. The house was razed before she was even born, so all she's ever seen are pictures. She's amazing at sorting through what we have to find gems of old photographs and documents. The woman is truly an asset here."

"An asset," I repeated, still a bit stunned.

Ann nodded. "Oh, yes. When she heard that Ms. Hostenfelder was looking about possibly getting a grant, she sprang into action. She's the one who insisted we go over there on Saturday and talk to Ms. Hostenfelder. She's determined not to see another historic farm completely fall to development."

"Which is why she's been out there every day, digging for relics to help Suzette with the grant applications," I mused.

Ann frowned. "What? Why would she do that? The grants Ms. Hostenfelder is applying for deal with farmland preservation and historic building maintenance. There wouldn't be any important artifacts, and if there were it wouldn't matter. The value of that property is the historic structure—the house—as well as the remaining land of the original farm. Not whatever old horseshoes or broken pottery might be half-buried in a field."

"You didn't know she has been out there every day this week?" I asked. "Didn't you notice her not coming in to work?"

"Miranda is part-time," Ann explained. "And she took this week off to deal with some unexpected family matters. I've got no idea why she'd spend the whole week digging up Ms. Hostenfelder's property. What on earth is she looking for out there?"

"Treasure." I pulled the pearl out of my pocket and unwrapped it, sitting it on the counter. "Have you ever seen Miranda wear something like this? And can you tell if it's a modern piece of jewelry or something old—say something that might date before the Civil War?"

She picked up the pearl, eyeing it carefully. "I've never seen Miranda wear pearls. She's not much of a jewelry person aside from some gold hoops or modest earrings. This looks like it might have been part of a necklace—and not the sort of necklace someone would wear casually either. As for its age, it looks old to me, but I'd need to have a jeweler look at it to actually date it."

"So fancy jewelry," I mused. "Not something a woman would wear if she intended on digging in a field during a cold March day."

Ann snorted out a laugh. "Uh, no. I don't know of many historians and archeologist who go out on digs wearing ornate pearl necklaces."

I took the pearl back from her, wrapping it and putting it back in my pocket. Then told Ann about the letters—the letters that she'd said Miranda had scanned. I told her about the looting, the possible buried treasure.

Ann scowled. "Even if Miranda hasn't found anything and kept it, she is still there under false pretenses, digging around Ms. Hostenfelder's property."

"I think she did find something," I told her. "Miranda was seen pulling a metal box out of the ground, and when I went to look at the area, I found that pearl in the dirt."

"That's inexcusable," Ann snapped. "If she found something on Monday, she's had days to report it. Clearly at this point whatever she found should be considered stolen."

"*And* she stole your drone," I added.

"I'm not sure we can prove that," Ann replied. "We don't have security cameras back here, and any footage from up front that showed Miranda, she could easily explain away. She worked here Thursday and was in the office scanning letters and going through old documents. I'd have no real proof that she took the drone."

"I wish there was a way we could find the controller for it," I mused. "I doubt we could get a warrant, and she probably either threw it away or has it safely hidden in her home somewhere."

"Or in her car," Ann said. "If she's digging on the property, she probably still has hopes of finding it, and replacing it along with the controller before anyone notices they're gone."

I nodded. Not that Miranda keeping the controller in her car would do me any good. I still wouldn't be able to get a warrant to search her car. Or test her shovel for DNA and blood. All I had was a stolen drone, proof that she'd lied about several things, and a pearl.

The pearl.

"There are two treasures," I told Ann. "I believe Miranda has already found one of them, but she's still looking for the other one, and I'm thinking it's buried somewhere near the pond."

I wondered if we set up a trap, told Miranda that Suzette was doing some preliminary work around the pond and found an old gold coin…

Just one coin. Or a piece of jewelry. Or a half-buried metal box that Suzette didn't want to disturb without having a historian or archeologist looking at it first. Once the trap was set, Suzette could pretend to go to work for the day, so that Miranda could swoop in and steal the treasure without anyone seeing her.

We'd watch and set up cameras and have this all recorded. At the very least we could get Miranda for fraud and theft, and then maybe the police would have enough evidence to test her shovel and possibly find hard evidence to connect her to Stan's murder.

"I'm wondering if you could do us a favor," I asked Ann. "I need an old metal box and some coins and other valuables to put into it. It's got to be real stuff, because Miranda would be able to tell the difference between something a decade or so old, and something that had been in the ground for over a hundred and fifty years."

"A box? Coins?" Ann's brows knitted together. "What are you going to do with them?"

"I'm going to bury them," I told her. "Everything will come back to you safe and sound, and if this goes well, we'll catch ourselves a thief."

A thief, and quite possibly a murderer.

CHAPTER 27

I spent the rest of the afternoon calling, texting, and making arrangements. As soon as I got home after work, I met the gang at Suzette's house, and we sprang into action. We worked until dark, placing the cameras that we'd borrowed from local hunters, as well as a few of the nature hobbyists in the neighborhood. They were positioned with great stealth on the old dock, the side of the house, the ancient chicken coop and the dilapidated barn. A few cameras we'd even set just a bit above ground level, hoping to catch a few angles the others might miss.

Checking the cameras's line of site, we decided on the spot where we should bury the box of treasure. One of Matt's friends had brought over a small Bobcat, clearing and turning up some ground near the pond before parking it nearby. We carefully hid the box in the area at the recent excavation.

"Think this will work?" Suzette asked Miles, who was supervising the whole endeavor.

"We'll definitely get her on theft," the deputy said. "Except for theft we need to get proof of her taking the loot off the property, then give her time for a reasonable person to report the find before arresting her."

Ann twisted her hands together. "How do we know she won't sell the stuff in the box? Or hide it somewhere? Those items belong to the museum, and I can't lose them."

"We have an inventory of the items in the box," Miles told her. "I can't guarantee that nothing will happen to them, but I'll do everything I can to safeguard the museum's property."

Ann blew out a breath. "It's to catch a thief, someone who betrayed my trust and stole from both the Historical Society and Ms. Hostenfelder. It's worth the risk."

"I want more than to get her on theft," Suzette said. "I want her charged with that man's murder. Maybe if I surprise her when she's retrieving the box, she'll try to kill me just as she did that surveyor."

Miles's eyes widened. "I can't let you risk yourself like that Ms Suzette."

"But what if Miranda *didn't* kill that man?" Ann asked. "Your approaching her means we might lose our chance to get her on theft."

"I agree with Miles and Ann," I said. "We should stick with the plan."

I understood Suzette wanting to prove Miranda was guilty of murder, but it wasn't worth her risking her life or screwing up the one crime we most definitely could get Miranda on.

Two shadowy spirits rose from the ground, flitting about the area near the pond. One young and dead long ago, the other a bit older and recently deceased. Neither ghost seemed aware of the other, but they were both agitated. As they fluttered around the edge of the pond, Stan's ghost passed through Ann and she shivered, wrapping her arms around herself.

"Is it going to snow again?" she commented, looking

toward the setting sun. "I just felt a chill even through my coat."

"I don't think so." Miles peered up at the sky. "But it has been an unseasonably cold March so far."

"So I'm supposed to send this picture to Miranda tomorrow morning?" Suzette asked, pulling up the photo of the spot where we'd buried the box on her phone and another of her holding a gold coin. "I tell her that I hired someone to begin restoration on the pond, and that they came across this when they were excavating. I had them stop and messaged her, worried that we might be disturbing an area of historic significance."

Miles nodded. "You said she usually gets here around nine in the morning, so text her a little before eight thirty. Let her know the excavators arrived here at eight, that you sent them home, and that you'll meet her here after work to show her the coin and the spot."

"Won't she know they did this tonight?" Suzette asked, waving a hand at the upturned soil. "The neighbors would confirm the Bobcat arrived tonight, that they heard it running tonight and not in the morning."

"Miranda isn't going to go interrogating the neighbors," Ann told her. "She'll take you at your word. She's greedy and wants the treasure, and won't be suspicious."

"I agree." I put a hand on Suzette's shoulder. "It'll be okay. And we'll all be nearby. Between us and the cameras, we'll catch her."

Suzette bit her lip and nodded. "Good. I'll meet you all here early tomorrow, then."

We all went home to wait for tomorrow. I was sure the others were just as anxious as I was. We had diner. The kids did their homework. The animals were taken care of, and no one seemed to notice how distracted I was until everyone had gone to bed and the judge and I began work at the dining room table as usual.

"Okay, Kay." Judge Beck sighed, pushing back from the table and closing the lid on his laptop. "Spill it. Something's been on your mind all night. I've never seen you so distracted before."

I told him everything—filling him in on what had happened in the last few days and what Miles, Suzette, Ann and I had planned for tomorrow morning.

"I don't like you being there, Kay," Judge Beck said. "This woman probably murdered the surveyor, and if that's the case, there's nothing stopping her from trying to do the same thing to you."

"Except I'll be up in the attic taking pictures," I assured him. "Miles is the one who will be down there hiding nearby. Although if everything goes according to plan, Miranda won't even see him. We're just there to document her stealing the treasure, not to confront her. Yet, anyway."

The judge thought about that for a second. "Okay. But take Cagney with you. And maybe a gun."

I laughed. "I don't have a gun. And even if I did, I'm not about to go shooting a thief and potential murderer in Suzette's backyard—a woman who is probably only armed with a shovel."

"Probably," the judge pointed out. "She's killed once. She might kill again. And this time she'll probably be better prepared to do so—which means *she* might be the one carrying a gun and not just a shovel."

He was right, but I still didn't see the risk in watching the whole thing from Suzette's second story window.

"I'm not taking Cagney, and I'm not taking a gun," I told him.

He got up and went to a drawer in the sideboard, pulling out something that looked like an asthma inhaler.

Putting it on the dining room table, he pushed it over to me.

"What the heck is this?" I asked, picking the item up.

"Pepper spray." He smiled. "It shoots a stream that reaches fifteen feet."

"Holy cow." I laughed. "That's pretty much the range of wasp spray."

He grinned. "I bought it for Madison, thinking it might be a good idea for her to carry it with her when she was walking Cagney, or if she was out with her friends at night. I'd like you to take it with you tomorrow. Just in case."

"Just in case I come across any wasps?" I teased.

"Just in case you come across any wasps with a gun, or a knife, or ninja skills," he said.

I looked at the container. There was a safety switch on the side, a plunger to depress for a spray of toxic mist, and a clip so the bottle could be carried on a belt or the waistband of a pair of pants.

"Okay," I said, figuring that this was better than the gun idea. It seemed silly to take this with me, but if it alleviated Judge Beck's worries, then I'd do it.

"Text me as soon as everything is in the clear?" he asked.

I smiled. "Absolutely."

* * *

Daisy and I skipped our yoga the next morning, instead converging with everyone at Suzette's house just before sunrise. Olive, Suzette, Me, Daisy, and Miles all crowded in Suzette's kitchen, drinking coffee and discussing the plan.

"I want everyone out of here as soon as she makes the call," Miles informed us.

"We know, we know. Olive and I are going to my house to wait it out," Daisy said, a bit unhappy at the fact that she wasn't going to remain at the cabin to watch. "And Suzette is going to go to work."

"Where I'll sit at my desk all day, biting my fingernails," Suzette finished.

We'd be biting our fingernails as well.

Suzette had a long driveway. Olive and Daisy would be able to see the front of the cabin and Miranda's car in the drive if they craned their necks looking out one of Daisy's windows, but that was it. I'd have a better view from Suzette's upstairs window, and be taking pictures from there. It was better than being halfway down the block trying to see from Daisy's house, but not by much. I wouldn't be involved in the action, although as I'd told Judge Beck the night before, if everything went well, there wouldn't be any action. We'd just get evidence of Miranda stealing the box with the treasure, then Miles would take it from there.

At least I'd be able to see what was going on. Taking photos of a woman digging wasn't exactly exciting investigative work. But if I'd discovered one thing this past year, a lot of investigative work wasn't all that exciting.

"I'll be watching," Miles reassured Suzette. He planned to hide near the old chicken coop, close enough to see what was going on and take his own pictures, just in case the cameras and I didn't catch everything.

Suzette pulled out her phone, took a few deep breaths, then started dialing, putting it to her ear when Miranda answered.

"Hi Miranda. Remember I said not to come out this morning because there was going to be excavating around the pond? Well, the guy no sooner got started when he stops and he tells me he found something. I'll send you a picture of it. It's a coin and it looks old. He also thinks there's something metal there that he scraped with the equipment. No, no, he didn't dig it up or anything. I had him go home because I was worried he might be messing up something of historical significance." Suzette listened for a few seconds, shooting Miles a quick glance before responding. "I need to leave for work and can't be late. I sent the excavator home. No, I still don't want you to come out today. It's too dangerous for you to work here alone. Two people have had accidents in that pond, and one of them died. Plus it's all muddy and slippery where he was digging. I don't want to risk anything happening to you when you're out here alone. Why don't I meet you here at four o'clock today? I'll show you the coin he dug up and we'll go look at the site together. It's probably nothing—probably just more of those hinges or other junk, but I didn't want to have him keep digging, in case there was something valuable there. Okay good. I'll see you then."

Suzette disconnected the call, sent the two pictures to Miranda via text, then wiped her hands on her pants. "Done. I'll go to work and wait for someone to call me."

"What if she doesn't show?" Daisy asked.

"Then we'll have to think of something else," I told her.

We'd assumed that Miranda would come during the day when Suzette was at work so she could find and take the box. Then she'd come back at four, and be just as disappointed as Suzette when they dug in the dirt and found nothing.

Miranda would be guilty of theft, and once Miles arrested her for that, he could get a warrant to find the other treasure, and possibly enough evidence to tie Miranda to the murder.

"You're not going to get in trouble for this, are you?" I asked Miles. "Toots is the detective in charge of the case. Won't you get in trouble for messing in his investigation?"

"Toots is investigating a murder. I'm here because a homeowner suspects someone is stealing," he replied.

I eyed him. "And the home is the same one where the murder occurred. I just don't want you losing your job over this, Miles. There are cameras set up all over the place. You can leave the watching to me. I'll handle it then file an official police report after the fact."

Miles shook his head. "I'm worried the camera footage might be blurry or a bad angle, or that you might not be able to see her with the box at all. Plus I'm a law enforcement officer. Me actually witnessing her take the box might make the difference between her getting away with theft and her getting arrested. If there's any fallout, I'll deal with it."

"Then after she leaves with the box?" Suzette asked.

"We wait a reasonable amount of time—until after your meeting with her at four. Then we'll get a warrant to search her house and car. We'll retrieve the items and arrest her for theft," Miles said.

It sounded straight-forward, but I was still worried. I kept thinking of all the things that could go wrong. What if Miranda hid the treasure somewhere before she got to her house and the search warrant turned up with nothing? Yes, there still would be Miles's testimony and the camera footage, plus whatever I could see from the upstairs window. And there would be Mr. Ambrose's testimony about seeing Miranda and Stan, as well as seeing Miranda unearth a box from near his apple tree where I'd found the pearl. But it all felt flimsy.

I headed upstairs with my camera, settling in a chair by Suzette's bedroom window. After about an hour, I heard a car pull in the driveway. I got up and went to the other bedroom that faced the front of the house, standing slightly to the side so I'd be hidden by the lacy curtains in case the woman happened to look up. Miranda got out of the vehicle, and after looking around, she came to the front door and rang the bell.

I held still, snapping a few quick pictures of her as I

waited it out. She was double checking that no one was home to see her. Smart.

Miranda rang the bell a few more times, then knocked on the door and peeked in the downstairs windows. Finally satisfied that no one was there, she went back to her car, pulled a shovel and a bag from her trunk, then headed to the backyard.

I made my way as quietly as possible back to Suzette's room and those windows. As I watched, Miranda dropped the bag on the ground, then began to poke around the turned-up dirt with her shovel. It took her around twenty minutes of searching to find where we'd hidden the box. Once she'd discovered it, Miranda got to work, and soon had removed the box from the ground.

I continued to take pictures as she put down her shovel, sat on the ground, and opened the box. With another quick look around, she took the bag from her back, and began to carefully place the contents of the box inside. When she was done, she began to rebury the box.

A sudden crash caught both of our attention. I jerked my camera over to the chicken coop. It had partially collapsed, the whole back half of it now angling sharply to the ground. Sucking in a breath, I hoped that Miles was okay, then I hoped that the noise wouldn't give us all away and ruin our sting operation.

Lowering the camera and looking back to where Miranda stood, I saw her staring at something. I followed her line of site, and saw she was looking directly at one of the cameras we'd mounted at the corner of the chicken coop. She put down her shovel and slowly headed in that direction.

Crap. There was no way for Miles to get out from behind the chicken coop without Miranda seeing him. Depending on his position, there was a chance he could hold still and she might not notice him, but I doubted it. She'd seen the camera. She'd want to look around and search for other cameras as well. And if she did that, she'd see Miles.

As I suspected, Miranda yanked the camera off the coop, then shoved it in a pocket. She walked around the side of the coop, stopping abruptly. Fearing Miles had been seen, I lifted my camera and zoomed in to get a better view.

That's when I saw the arm. Miles had definitely been seen, but from the position of his arm and the lack of movement, I realized the coop must have fallen on him, trapping him and possibly even knocking him out.

Miranda stared down at the deputy for a second, then grabbed another camera off that side of the chicken coop. As she shoved it in her pocket, she walked back to where she'd found the box, and picked up her shovel.

I was positive she'd killed Stan, and watching her pick up that shovel, I knew right away that she intended to do the same thing to Miles. Without a second thought, I threw my camera on the bed and ran down the stairs, hoping to get to Miles before she did.

I couldn't see either of them from ground-level, but I ran through the backyard, moving as quickly as I could through the weeds toward the chicken coop. I'd been in such a hurry that I'd neglected to take anything I could use as a weapon, but I remembered the pepper spray that Judge Beck had insisted I carry, and grabbed the cannister from my belt, clicking off the safety. Rounding the corner of the chicken coop, I saw Miranda standing over an unconscious Miles, her shovel raised.

"Stop," I shouted. Then I let loose with the pepper spray.

The stream nailed Miranda right in the face. She screamed, dropping the shovel and frantically clawing at her eyes. I didn't let up, emptying the container on her, and kicking the shovel away when I was close enough.

She swung a wild hand at me, then took off, stumbling

and cursing as she ran through the weeds toward the house and her car. I knelt down to check on Miles. He groaned opening his eyes, then lifting a hand to his head.

"You okay?" I waited for his nod, then took off for the house, pulling out my phone and dialing 911. We'd need help getting that chicken coop off of Miles, and he probably needed to at least be checked out for a concussion.

Just as the 911 operator answered, I heard the sounds of barking, and a scream.

"We have an officer in need of medical attention, and—" My voice trailed off as I came around the side of the house and got a good look at the scene in front of me. Miranda had her back pressed against the driver's door of her car, her hands raised, her eyes and face red and tear-streaked from the pepper spray. Olive and Daisy stood at angles, blocking any avenue of escape. And holding the woman in place with some truly fierce barking were Lady and Gus.

Suzette, Olive and I hovered over the blueprints while Gus and Cagney romped around her backyard.

"The pond restoration begins tomorrow," Suzette said. "The new dock will go here, and I want a reconstruction of the waterfowl nesting box here."

"She's wants to rebuild the chicken coop, and the old barn as well," Olive said, pointing to the spots on the plans where the outbuildings were marked.

"That's only if the second grant comes in," Suzette reminded her.

"And the orchard?" I asked, looking down at the papers.

"That's if next month's fundraiser goes well," Suzette commented, holding up her crossed fingers.

With the grant award covering the pond restoration, and a potential second grant to cover the outbuildings, Suzette had shifted her attention to the three acre field. She hoped to raise enough money to pay for the apple orchard.

She had also signed away that contested ten foot strip of land to the property owners on Broad Street, and in return, they'd all donated to her renovations. That money, plus a generous discount from a local company had meant Suzette would finally have her fence.

After Miranda had been arrested, a search warrant on her house had discovered the box she'd dug up from the back field. The pearl I'd found had been a match for a necklace discovered in the box—a necklace with a missing pearl.

Suzette had donated the coins and jewelry to several museums, saying that she didn't feel right profiting from what was stolen property. We'd yet to find the treasure that Orvil planned to bury near where the geese's nesting box had once stood. Maybe we'd find it once the pond restoration started. Maybe we'd never find it. If we did, Suzette planned to donate that treasure as well.

"The pond work should be done by late April—just in time for the fundraising event," Suzette said as she rolled up the plans.

She was excited about the event, looking forward to sharing the history of her family farm with the community. If it was a success, she was considering making it an annual happening, with future years' funds going to the Locust Point Historical Society who would provide grants for other restoration projects in the community. Suzette, Ann from the Historical Society, Matt, and Madison were in charge of organizing the event, and Madison was particularly excited to be taking a leadership role in her first fundraising activity.

The search warrant on Miranda's house hadn't just turned up the stolen treasure. The police had found some blood trace on her shovel, and clothing with blood on it as well. The lab confirmed that it was Stan's blood, and that plus Mr. Ambrose's statement added murder to her long list of charges. Miles had been okay except for a mild concussion and some bruised ribs from where the chicken coop had fallen on him, and although Detective Toots wasn't the deputy's biggest fan, Miles hadn't gotten in trouble for our sting operation.

The best news of all was that Travis was out of the hospital. The boy was already insisting he was well enough to resume his paper route and after school job at the arcade. We were on week two of the meal train, and tonight was my night to deliver a casserole, salad, and a chocolate cake to their house.

"I'm looking forward to a swim in your pond this summer," I told Suzette.

"Absolutely," she replied. "I plan on hosting a few parties, too. I've got to build some goodwill because in a few years, I'll need everyone's help for apple harvesting."

"Sounds like fun." It did. I was looking forward to baking some of those apples as well. Apple pie. Apple dumplings. Fried apples. Applesauce.

And I still wanted to find the recipe for Gertrude's Walnut Jubilee Pie. I had a feeling that this was going to be a year of pies. Pies, friends, family, love, and community. A woman couldn't ask for more than that.

ACKNOWLEDGMENTS

Thanks to Lyndsey Lewellen for cover design and typography, and to Kim Cannon for copyediting. And special thanks to all my readers who love Kay and her friends. Read, bake, snuggle your Taco, and take a chance on love.

ABOUT THE AUTHOR

Libby Howard lives in a little house in the woods with her sons and two exuberant bloodhounds. She occasionally knits, occasionally bakes, and occasionally manages to do a load of laundry. Most of her writing pre-COVID was done in a pub where she could combine work with people-watching, a decent micro-brew, and a plate of Old Bay wings. But lately it's all about pajamas and the couch.

For more information:
libbyhowardbooks.com/

<u>Locust Point Mystery Series:</u>

The Tell All

Junkyard Man

Antique Secrets

Hometown Hero

A Literary Scandal

Root of All Evil

A Grave Situation

Last Supper

A Midnight Clear

Fire and Ice

Best In Breed

Cold Waters

Five for a Dollar - coming in 2022

Lonely Hearts - coming in 2022

* * *

<u>Reckless Camper Mystery Series - coming in 2022</u>

The Handyman Homicide

Death is on the Menu

The Green Rush

Elvis Finds a Bone